nailed

ALSO BY PATRICK JONES

Things Change

nailed

PATRICK JONES

WALKER & COMPANY ✸ NEW YORK

To my mom, Betty Jones, and in memory of my father,
Vaughn Paul Jones, who never hammered, always encouraged,
and provided me with love, support, and my first typewriter.

First published in the United States of America in 2006 by
Walker Publishing Company, Inc.
Distributed to the trade by Holtzbrinck Publishers

For information about permission to reproduce selections from this
book, write to Permissions, Walker & Company, 104 Fifth Avenue,
New York, New York 10011.

Library of Congress Cataloging-in-Publication Data

Jones, Patrick.
Nailed / Patrick Jones.
p. cm.
Summary: An outcast in a school full of jocks, sixteen-year-old Bret
struggles to keep his individuality through his interest in drama and music,
while trying to reconnect with his father.
ISBN-10: 0-8027-8077-6
ISBN-13: 978-0-8027-8077-5
[1. Self-perception—Fiction. 2. Fathers and sons—Fiction.
3. High schools—Fiction. 4. Schools—Fiction.] I. Title.
PZ7.J7242Nai 2006   [Fic]—dc22   2005027447

Visit Walker & Company's Web site at
www.walkeryoungreaders.com

Printed in the United States of America

2 4 6 8 10 9 7 5 3 1

All papers used by Walker & Company are natural, recyclable products made
from wood grown in well-managed forests. The manufacturing processes
conform to the environmental regulations of the country of origin.

ACKNOWLEDGMENTS

Thanks to the folks who read early version of *Nailed* and whose comments helped me construct a better book: Amy Alessio, Brent Chartier, Sarah Cornish, Kristin Dziczek, Paula Hoffman, Rosemary Honnold, David Lane, Renée Vaillancourt McGrath, Angela Pfeil, Jessica Mize, Patricia Taylor, and Tricia Suellentrop. Thanks to Sara Swenson and the teens in the manuscript discussion group she organized at Edina (MN) High School. Special thanks to teen readers Ashley, Nikki, Kaitlin, and Amber who read the manuscript and provided me with invaluable suggestions. Thanks to Larry O. Dean (www. larryodean.com) who allowed me to use his song titles. Kudos to Ken Rasak for his important contribution to this book, and to Erica Klein for her important contribution to this book, and my life. Finally, with belated thanks to Doug Dixon, my high school drama teacher, for everything he did for me and other students.

nailed

One

Bret, what the hell is wrong with you?"

I stand mute for a moment as my dad shakes his head. "What do you mean?" I reply, playing Mr. Innocent without much conviction.

"Why don't you go inside with the women?" my dad says in a voice that kills. "Go bake cookies with your mother or play dolls with your sister, Robin."

I don't say anything, because words don't matter. What matters is changing the oil filter on Mom's car. I turned sixteen yesterday, and with my new driver's license I was ready to burn up summer on the road, except my father imposed rules not required by Michigan's secretary of state. It wasn't enough that I knew how to drive, there were other conditions to be met before I would be allowed to take Mom's molting Geo Metro onto Flint's freeways. There was no way he'd give me the keys to his old NASCAR bumper sticker tattooed black pickup, and he wouldn't even let me stand within ten feet of his vintage red Camaro Beretta, which he paid more attention to than me. To get the rights to Mom's Metro rust ride I had to show him I could maintain her car. I could change a tire, but that wasn't enough. He wanted me to show him I could change the oil. This wasn't a class they taught—or that I would take—at Southwestern High School.

"Why can't I just use the car, like everyone else?" I ask, but he never listens. He just stares at my green-tinted ponytail and the goofy Goodwill clothes draped over my lanky and ludicrously unathletic six-foot frame, gazing at an offspring he's embarrassed to be seen with, let alone admit to siring. He's in his usual dull gray grease-stained coveralls.

Laughing, he shakes his head, and grunts, "Stop whining and do like I showed you." In the driveway, he's teaching me the hard way, his way, the only way. He hands me the oil filter and points. "It goes there. It fits right in."

He turns away to light up another Marlboro while I just stare at the car's engine. Changing the tires, stuff on the outside, that was easy, but stuff on the inside was a lot more complicated. I'm A-student smart, so I could learn to do this, but I won't give my dad the satisfaction of making me. I'll walk everywhere or catch a ride with my buds and band mates, Alex and Sean. I'll do anything; anything other than this thing Dad wants me to do.

"Guess Mr. Douglas doesn't teach you this in theater class," he says, rubbing in his disdain like grease into his coveralls. His eyes avoid me, they are asking his ongoing but unsaid question being, "What do you think you're doing with yourself?"

I have no reply, and can only shrug. My dad and I never talk anymore, and this is why.

"You don't learn this in books," he adds, angry that I was still up reading (*The Grapes of Wrath*) at 5:00 a.m. when he got up for work, knowing it would mean I'd sleep in until noon, which ticked him off. But that's his fault too; he and Mom were yelling at each other late into the night, so I ducked under the covers and behind the headphones, letting the loud sounds of *London Calling* by punk patriarchs The Clash drown them out.

"Not in the classics," I say under my breath. All Dad ever reads are car magazines, the sports section, and the Sunday comics.

"Jesus H. Christ, Bret, this is a simple task." He almost spits out the words. Unsaid is that my older brother, Cameron, would be able to do it. In fact, Cam did this particular task so well that he now does oil changes for a living. If you call that living; there's a lot of that in Flint.

Again, more silence from me. I don't know what I'm supposed to say. When I'm acting on stage, I can ad lib if needed because I know who the characters are, but in real life I can't figure out my or my father's character. To him, I'm some alien life-form holed up in his house.

"Bret, why do you always want to do things the hard way?" my father asks, but the question is rhetorical, not that he knows what that word means. "Your mom can't protect you forever. You need to learn to do stuff for yourself."

"Why do I need to learn to change the oil?" I ask, not as a challenge, but out of a desperate need to know why something so small matters so much. To him and to me.

"Because."

I wait for the rest of the sentence, but it doesn't come as he backs away from me.

"Because I said so." He finally finishes the sentence, and the conversation. Throwing his smoke onto the driveway, he walks back into the garage and his tabernacle of tools, returning to work on another project, once again giving up on me. I put my headphones back on and close the hood of the car, ending my chance of driving and resembling a normal sixteen-year-old.

I retreat toward my room, while my father starts hammering away at the gun rack he's building for his hunting rifle, a new pawn shop purchase. The loud pounding breaks through the wall of sound in my Discman. I walk away realizing I surrendered my chance at being normal a long time ago. As I look over my shoulder back toward the garage, I see, hear, but mostly feel the thumping as my father slams the heavy hammer against the skinny nails. He's not just building something or tearing me down. He's also teaching me yet another angry lesson that I'm too stubborn to learn: the nail that sticks out farthest gets hammered hardest.

Two

Alex, why are we driving ourselves crazy like this?"

"Drive? I thought you weren't allowed to drive," Alex cracks back. It's his typical smartass statement. "Crazy is within walking distance for us."

Alex Shelton, my best pal, sits on a bench with me in front of the theater at Genesee Valley Mall. We pass a Camel cig between us, watching half the world go by. The better half.

"She's a seven," I say as we spy a gorgeous Gothwannabe girl, clad in black skirt and tight black T-shirt, walking by on the outskirts of her group of friends. Alex and I started this girl-rating ritual on a trip to Stratford, Ontario, for a Shakespeare festival. The number represents the number of fingers or toes we would sacrifice to any deity who could arrange for us to spend horizontal time with these unattainable angels.

"She's for you," Alex responds, yet I know none of these ladies will look at me, then simply smile. Just as well, since most of my crushes end in crushing disappointment after weeks or months of flirtation. Except for Megan the Imposter, who crushed me a whole different way last spring.

"In my dreams," I reply. We know Rule One is that no guy is ever less good-looking than the girl he's with. We keep searching for, but not finding, duos where homely horny toads like us couple with killer lookers. My fellow troglodytes must stay underground, while blond-haired blue-eyed beautiful boys like Sean, our band's drummer, roam the earth. Sean's a near ten among men, while Alex, challenged in vertical reach and clear skin, and I strive to be fives. Math may be my worst subject, but even I understand the awful arithmetic of animal attraction: guys who are fives like me don't get girls who are tens.

Rule Two is to find the outsider. Every group has an odd one out, like our gorgeous Goth girl, and that's the one we make our focus. We figure since every other wolf pack ignores the outsider, we will flatter her with attention, even if it's from a safe distance.

Rule Three is to never make eye contact. That is the difference between those of us who appreciate the captivating splendor of the female form from a respectful distance and the rude, crude bullyboys with stalker tendencies. We want love but settle for lust, or even just a look.

"Nine," Alex says, slapping my knee as a Mona Lisa Cheerleader, a girl from our school who remains unattainable to all but members of the jockarchy, walks by. The jockarchy is what we call the ball-bouncing bloc at school. Bob Hitchings, a former elementary school friend who now punches me for kicks and ridicules Alex like it was an Olympic event, is the three-letter king of that hill. At our school, these knuckle draggers score points and win rewards, but from most of us in theater, they earn only our scorn and ridicule. It's not just that they kick the ball; it's that they seem to think they deserve to walk on water and stomp on those less privileged. They're so admired at school that standing up to them isn't an option; it's a daydream.

"Very nine," I add.

"Bret, my pants are getting tighter," Alex whispers.

"No wonder they call it longing," I say. Alex cracks up. We want love and would settle for lust, but we have to make do with making each other laugh with bad puns and quick comebacks.

"Get the blood back into your brain," he says, snapping his fingers off my skull.

"Do you think they know we're doing this? Are we that obvious?" I ask.

"We should wear sunglasses," Alex says as he puts on a pair of shades to match his similar green-streaked (but naturally blond) hair, and the gold rims balance his numerous silver earrings. The sunglasses fit, since Alex is always the star of the show. He's arrogant, but he's also the smartest and funniest person I know, and a damn good friend. He's also a first-class secondhand store shopper. Today's getup is typical: the oversized black pants, a Captain Crunch T-shirt, and like me, bright green Chuck Taylor Converse All Stars; basketball shoes for two guys who can't dribble or dunk. We both prefer to hit the hardwood of the stage rather than the gym, where the pituitary cases that make up the starting five of the Flint Southwestern Spartans bang bodies. Whether it's not having a dad that beats him down, his distaste for people who don't share his taste, or his lack of fear in the face of adversity, Alex mostly avoids the problems I have swimming upstream against the high school gene pool.

"Then we'd be cool, like Sean," I say. Sean should be part of the jockarchy like his neighbor Bob Hitchings, but he's not. It's not really about sports aptitude, but a superior attitude. Sean's common love of radio-unfriendly music, smartass comments, and offbeat books and movies makes him one of us. Besides, he and Alex go way back, and loyalty matters.

"I bet those girls wouldn't even care," Alex says. "They'd prefer the validation of their beauty over the invasion of their privacy. They're all beautiful, someone should tell them. I tell you Mr. Bret Hendricks, there's not a girl in the world who isn't beautiful in some way."

"Especially Kylee Edmonds," I say. "So, Alex, tell me, what do you think Kylee is?"

He pauses to think. I've thrown him between the rock and the hard place. I'll watch him squirm while I wait for the next eye harem to pass. He takes the smoke from me and stalls.

Kylee is everything. During summer theater, Mr. Douglas invited students from Flint Central to team up for a play with us Westies. She told me she was a big deal over there, having starred in their musicals the last two years. But since we're doing *The Odd Couple,* with no singing or dancing, she opted to run the show behind the scenes as stage manager. If only she would opt for me, and let me hang on her arm like her twenty-bracelet parade.

A year older, Kylee is cynical, sarcastic, and sexy beyond belief. Petite, with a dancer's sexy body, she has a fondness for too-small tank tops and tight hip-hugging cutoffs, allowing for maximum skin exposure. This girl from Central knows how to center attention on herself, and I've gladly noticed her every second of every minute of every day. She was easy to find as the only person involved in the production with short, violet hair and a bottom lip like a plum. She never walks; she glides gracefully across the stage. Kylee's beauty is organic, original, and unbearable. After our final show in two weeks, there'll be a cast party and I'll need to make a move or lose my chance to know her. She'll be back at Central and on the outskirts of my life.

"Depends who is doing the rating," Alex finally says, but I

know he thinks that's Kylee's a total ten. Alex noticed her first but backed off, like a true trustworthy friend, once I expressed a passionate (rather than passing) interest. "I know what she is for you."

"What a succubus suck-up you are. Okay, she's a ten," I confess.

"I don't think so," Alex replies in his most annoying singsong put down voice.

"What, she's not a ten?" I ask nervously, the need for his approval noticeable.

"For you, she's a twenty!" he shouts.

"Twenty? That's all my fingers and toes! No wonder figuring out a way to approach her has me stumped!" I crack back, then we low-five. "Did you find out about a boyfriend?"

"Yes and no," Alex replies, disturbingly delighted by my discomfort.

"And?"

"Yes, she has a boyfriend," Alex says, looking away from me at the sky above, while my heart sinks six feet underground. "But I don't think she would be opposed to your advances."

"And tell me how you can predict that, Nostra-dumbass?"

"Her boyfriend's some college guy named Chad Lake."

"So what?" I ask, literally moving toward the edge of my seat.

"Well, she said, and I quote, 'He's less like a lake and more like a puddle.'"

"What does that mean?" I ask, knowing it will be Kylee-style: smart and sarcastic.

"She said he's more like a puddle because he's shallow and casts a nice reflection," Alex says, cracking us both up and drawing unwanted attention to our observation outpost, just as a major ten passes. I hear my heart beat faster, pumping blood south, as

I point the girl out to him. This girl is like a flag: red hair, white T-shirt, and blue jeans. She makes us stand at attention.

"I didn't realize you liked redheads," Alex comments.

"Don't you know by now what kind of girls I like?"

"None, if you ask your dad!" Alex chortles. My dad thinks both Alex and I are gay.

"I don't ask my dad anything," I say sharply. Alex's dad died when he was ten, and I never tell him how much I envy him for that; almost as much as I envy his ability to write songs.

"Well, you don't seem to have one type," Alex says, stating the obvious.

"I like redheads, blonds, brunettes, and Goths with black hair. Of late, I find that I'm especially interested in dancers with violet hair, and I'm sure if I saw a bald girl go by I would find something to like about her."

"I'll be on the lookout for one of those," Alex says with a sly grin.

"You think girls do this?" I ask, trying to distract myself.

"I hope not. We're not tens by any means," he says, stating the vicious and the obvious.

"Well, except for Sean," I acknowledge.

"Maybe our band should be called the Blond Shy Guy and the Multicolored Mangy Miscreants rather than Radio-Free Flint," Alex says.

"Maybe," I mutter, totally befuddled by the unfairness of beauty.

"Or how about the Mental Babes?" Alex cracks, but I don't respond. Last spring, there was a story about the theater club in the school paper. There was a quote from this popular-crowd girl, Becca Levy, calling me a "mental babe." I'm a successful student, an improving actor, a kick-ass bass player and energetic lead singer in my band. I try to be a good brother to my younger sister, Robin, even though she's twelve now and wants nothing to do with her weird older brother. Despite my problems with Dad at home and Bob Hitchings at school, the last few years have been a sweet life. But this "mental babe" memory sours me. It hurts even more coming from Becca, who, like me, is smarter than she is pretty. I've secretly always had a hard spot for her. Mental babe? Kill me now.

"I bet Kylee thinks that about me too," I say sadly, just as Sean joins us. Looking at Sean, I wonder if I was more like him and less like Alex, if I'd have more of a chance with Kylee.

"What, you don't think any girl would lose a finger over you?" Alex asks.

"Most just give me the finger," I say with a laugh.

Sean jabs me in the ribs, then points at a blond walking by. "She's tenriffic!"

Three

Don't miss your cue, cutie," Kylee reminds me as I take my place backstage, getting ready for a curtain call.

We've just finished our last show of the summer, but right now that doesn't matter. The only *Odd Couple* I'm thinking about is me and Kylee, and her tiny hands dancing over my skinny body. As I get ready to take my bow, I tip my hat and shoot her my best smile.

"See you at the cast party?" I ask, trying to mask my terror. Standing onstage in front of hundreds is easy compared to this audience of one. Two, if Chad waits in the wings.

"I'm bringing my dancing shoes," Kylee says, pointing for me to go onstage. After soaking up audience appreciation, I retreat from the stage into the dressing room. I take off my stage makeup, knowing I've made up my mind about Kylee: now or never; death or glory.

I hop into Alex's car, a beaten-up brown Crown Victoria, and the music is booming.

"This will be our first song at our first gig," Alex says over the funk-punk racket. I sink back into the broken seat, letting the music surround us while memories swallow me.

nailed

In junior high, I didn't have a girlfriend. Those horrible dances—boys on one side, girls on the other—made us all look like we were waiting for a firing squad to put us out of our misery. There was this one girl I liked, Debbie Wylie, but nothing ever happened. Other guys at school bragged in far too much detail about their schoolyard kisses, and the occasional anatomy excursions, but I never had a story to tell. I felt left out as everyone was pairing up but me. I was clumsy, skinny, and a little strange. My body's battled me since birth. Allergies, asthma, and severe-enough-for-surgery ear infections were my primary afflictions, and my body won every battle during junior high.

Freshman year of high school, the heart stopper and heart-breaker was Teresa Donaldson. I tried funny, and I tried serious. I tried paying attention to her, and I tried ignoring her. We had a great teasing thing going in a couple of classes, but I couldn't really break through. Then came my ill-fated attempt at high school wrestling, which ended up giving me more bruises than a box of dropped peaches at the Save-A-Lot grocery store. I was a mess. I can't say I blame Teresa for being cool to me. While I was often sweaty—an unfortunate result of wrestling other guys and not her—I was by no definition of the word *hot*.

While my new buds and future band mates Alex and Sean were both exploring various and sundry female forms, I was again on the outside looking in. The more isolated I felt from the great mating rituals taking place around me, the more I followed Alex's lead and grew more outrageous in dress and behavior. What I was doing wasn't working, so I thought I would try something else, something wild. If I were the center of attention, then someone would have to notice me. I don't mind being alone, but I hate feeling lonely and disconnected, a need even good friends can't fill.

In tenth grade, I just remember being "obsexed" all year. I looked at my teachers who wore wedding rings, and I remember thinking how they got to have sex all the time, even though they were pretty damn dull and uninteresting, so why not me? Instead, I was surfing Internet porn, seeking out real girls without success, and strengthening my left arm. I was fully convinced that I was too much of an outsider to ever get inside a girl, until I hooked up with Megan the Imposter.

Sophomore year I also got into Goth, to Alex's chagrin, which led to me finally getting some. Southwestern is big, and I don't remember even seeing Megan when we were both freshmen. But by sophomore year, her Goth attitude and attire attracted my attention. We started off by teasing, which turned into tickling, which burned into touching, and then more, although at a glacial pace.

I loved her even if I never said those words to her, but hated to learn that she came to school Mom-approved, then Gothed-up in the bathroom. We mostly saw each other at school and talked on the phone, but I never went over to her place or met her parents. She'd come over to my house, always when no one was home, where we'd partly undress for sexual success. This past spring, we were at Genesee Valley locking lips when her dad arrived on the scene. I don't know if it was fate or if he followed us, but did he ever freak at seeing this vampirelike version of his daughter swapping spit with his worst nightmare. He pulled her aside, told me to go back to hell, and then drove her back to Blandland. My phone calls went unreturned, and a few days later at school, her true preppy self emerged from her camouflage cocoon. She was posing while I was looking for the real thing. My mood turned as black as my fingernail polish. Even though I'd etched Megan's name into my then black-painted fingernails—one letter per finger on my right hand—she listened to the head of the family rather than her heart, scratching me off her list. After all these years of rejection, I don't know why I shouldn't expect the same from Kylee.

"So, what do you think?" Alex says as the song ends and I snap back into the present.

"Off the hook," I say, burying my envy at his songwriting prowess. We drive, but I'm listening to my own thoughts more than Alex's rants against the corporate music machine.

As we enter the party, Alex puts out his radar for any South-western alumni in attendance. He's convinced that high school girls just don't "get him," so he's looking for someone older. He's been flirting all summer with Elizabeth, this funky waitress at our after-band-practice pit stop the Venus, to no avail. I wish him luck, then head toward the music booming up the basement stairs. I see Kylee wearing a men's large white shirt like a dress, dancing with a group of her girls, oblivious to anything but the music in her head. I'm oblivious to anything but the effect of the music on her hips, and its effect on me. Chad Puddle isn't on site, so it's sink or swim. I feel my heart thump in my chest, while other muscle reactions are occurring at a lower level when she takes off the shirt, revealing a skintight tangerine leotard top. I tug nervously on my tie-dye Dr. Seuss T-shirt and take a giant step.

I throw no elbows as I dance through the girls-only crowd toward her. Her face lights up even in the darkness. Kylee bites her big bottom lip, nods, smiles, and moves like heaven.

We dance more, and share a few cigarettes, cloves for her, Camels for me. Kylee ignites each smoke using her kitschy Dr. Evil lighter from *Austin Powers*. After she lights one just for herself, she takes my hat and places it on her head, scooping up her red shoes on the way out of the room. I pursue her outside on the porch.

"Nice hat," she says, touching the brim of the fedora I've taken from the costume closet. It covers up her violet head.

"It looks better on you than me."

"You think?" Kylee replies, lightly touching my skinny arm with those tiny fingers.

"I know," I say quickly, tired of waiting for love to find me.

"Can I keep it?" She takes another drag, while I watch her lungs do their work.

"Sure, if . . ."

"If what?"

"If you'll go out with me." I deliver the line like a pro, even if I'm shaking inside.

"Like nudge-nudge, wink-wink?" Kylee asks, showing a smirky smile brighter than the stars above and making a Monty Python's Flying Circus reference to sex. MPFC is another intersection of our interests we'd discovered over the past month of pre-mating practice.

I hesitate, as a blush flowers across my face. "Nothing like that."

"Too bad." She shrugs and looks away.

I put my hand on her shoulder. It feels nice. "Okay, maybe a little of that."

"So, you're asking me out?"

"Well, I know you already have a boyfriend and all, but—"

"He's not really a boy or a friend," Kylee says with a wicked smile-and-wink combo.

"So, what do you think about you and me?"

"Can I ask you something first?" Kylee replies, chilling my spine.

"Anything."

"What took you so damn long?" she asks as she puts the hat back on my head.

"Well, I-I—" I'm stammering like a newbie on opening night.

"I thought you were gay like most of the theater guys at Central," she says, laughing. I wonder if she's been talking to my dad or Bob Hitchings. She moves closer, brushing her body up against mine, giving off a small shock while sparking a flutter from head to toe. "I mean, what else does a girl like me have to do? I was trying to bump into you all summer."

"Considering how clumsy I am, I'm surprised I didn't fall all over you first."

She's smart, sexy, and sarcastic, and I'm scared shitless. She finishes the last drag on her cigarette. "What's with your look?"

This is my summer of great fashion experimentation, as I reject my sophomore-year Goth and Megan-inspired black state, for every goofy T-shirt that Alex and I could acquire at the Goodwill during its two-for-one sale, and never finding time to go Gap-ing with Sean.

"You no like?" I bow toward her, then tip my hat.

"It's fine to see a guy wear a hat that's not a baseball cap turned backward or a hooded sweatshirt. Central is full of wannabes, not real deals," she says. "It sure gets you noticed."

"Not my intention."

She puts the pinky finger of her left hand against that luscious bottom lip. "Riiiiiiiiiight," she says, nailing a perfect Dr. Evil impersonation.

"Well, not everybody likes it," I say, understating the facts. "Like my boss."

"Where do you work?" Kylee asks.

"Sometimes I usher at the Whiting Auditorium, downtown," I tell her. It's a sweet gig that my drama teacher, Mr. Douglas, set up for me.

"That's right by my house," Kylee says. "My parents go to every benefit there."

"I just waltz people into their seats," I say, trying too hard to be too funny.

"I've danced on that stage myself many times," Kylee says with pride, then starts twirling around, showing off her skills and sexiness. "Our dance troupe is doing something there in a few weeks. Do you want to come watch us? It'll be fun."

"You really like to dance, don't you?" I ask her.

"Always, but you need to have the right shoes," she says as I look down and notice she's wearing bright red shoes that look like something from a production of The Wizard of Oz.

"You're wearing ruby slippers?" I ask, astonished and enthralled in the same instant. I have memorized her wardrobe, mentally cataloged it, even made predictions and hoped for certain outfits, but these ruby red slippers were blinding.

"I love wearing stuff from the prop room at Central. It's about half of my wardrobe throughout the school year," she says in the tone of spilling a secret.

"Hey, I've been using my school's costume room as my closet for the past year!"

"Well, Mr. Bret Hendricks, it seems we have quite a lot in common," she says, leaning toward me. "Except one little thing."

"And what's that?"

"You're a better actor. I sing almost as good as you, but I mostly just dance," she says, acting out the words by twirling around, making my head spin. "I wish I were as good as you."

nailed

"No one ever said that to me before," I reply, amazed.

"Oh, don't gimme that modesty crap," Kylee says, breaking out her biggest smile yet. "You know you're good, don't deny it. Bret Hendricks, you'd stand out in any crowd."

"Why's that?" I ask as I move closer.

"Because you're like me: the real thing," she replies, removing my hat and all my doubts. Our lips touch, and I know I'm not in Kansas—or my father's Flint—anymore.

Four

et your lazy butt out of bed!"

I ignore my father's angry voice with both ears, but open one eye to spy the clock radio's red numbers bright as the morning sun. It's 10:30 and he expects me to be laboring today.

"You got chores," my father says, getting my attention by softly kicking the side of my bed. Even if I felt like easily rising out of bed, my appearance is too hard and raised for that.

"It's my last free day before school, let me sleep," I mumble, hoping he won't hear me.

"Ain't no such thing as a free day," he quickly counters. "I've already worked five hours today while your lazy butt has been in bed."

"I'm working tonight," I counter meekly, thinking more how my real work begins tomorrow. School isn't work, it's fun; facing another year of Bob Hitchings is what tenses me up.

"Tough job, usher. No wonder you're exhausted," he says, then snorts. Dad uses phlegm as punctuation. "Look at me when I talk to you!"

"Let me sleep," I say, stalling and silently seeking blood redistribution.

"What the hell time did you get to bed last night?" He kicks the bed again, harder; angrier. The bed shakes: he must be wearing his heavy work boots.

If only I could tell him the truth: I got to bed early. I was in bed by 9:30, but then I'd have to tell him the whole truth: it wasn't my bed and I wasn't alone. Part of me wants to stand up for a little show-and-tell: "I'm straight!" then bring in Kylee as an expert witness. Instead, I try to push down thoughts of Kylee, of last night and our first time, as I figure out a way to escape my father's daily declarations of my laziness and constant disapproval of my life.

"I expect the lawn mowed by four," he says. Most days this summer he's come home for a quick lunch since his work—the Top Hat Car Wash—is only a mile or so away. Yet, I suspect his real mission isn't food, but harassing my hide. I thought on the last day before school, I'd get to sleep past noon, but Dad's stricter than Southwestern's principal, Mr. Morgan.

"But Alex, Sean, and I are shopping at Jellybean—" I lay out my facts, knowing that any sentence that begins with "but" never ends without mine getting metaphorically kicked.

"You listen to me and your mother, not your weird friends." More phlegm, more friction.

Alex is persona non grata at my house. In my father's eyes, I was more or less a normal kid until Alex and I hooked up in ninth grade, meeting in a creative writing class. In Alex, I found somebody who laughed at the same jokes, liked the same music, and felt the same disdain for the jockarchy.

"And I expect this pigsty to be cleaned when I get home," he says, adding a final kick to the bed, a few loud stomps, then a door slam to finish his parental-rage percussion solo.

I wait to hear the front door lock, the sound of Dad's truck starting, and finally feel the safety of knowing he's on his way to work to let off his steam on dirty cars instead of his kids. His kid: he never yells at Robin, and I don't seem to recall him riding Cam, but then again, they both turned out how he wanted by fitting in and not causing him any trouble.

"Mom! Robin! Are you here?" I shout. When I hear nothing but silence, I return to thoughts of last night with Kylee, reliving the feeling and relieving the pressure down below under the sheets, except it's not fantasy anymore; now it's a fantastic memory.

I clean up with a quick shower and proceed to clean up my room in a way that my "Mister Place for Everything" father would hate. I heave my horizontal closet pile of Southwestern costume room castoffs and thrift store treasures under the bed, shove my secondhand books, CDs, and videos in boxes, then stack those in the closet, and pack into my desk the piles of papers filled with unfinished songs.

Next, I start to mow the lawn, decked out in my fedora, torn-and-frayed black Austin 3:16 T-shirt, and green fatigues. I get about half of it done when I'm interrupted by Robin and her giggling girlfriends riding their bikes into the driveway. I turn the mower off and greet them.

"What's up, Ro?" I say, shooting a friendly wave to her, which she doesn't return.

She looks through me, as if she's embarrassed I'm talking to her. She turns her back, whispers something to her friends, who all break out in laughter, no doubt at my expense.

"What's so funny my fair ladies?" I say in an English accent while tipping my hat.

"You are so weird," Robin says slowly, making sure her friends savor each word.

"And you're so rude," I mutter under my breath. I want to tell her she didn't think I was weird when I helped her learn to ride that bike, played endless board games with her, or read her hundreds of library books. I want to say all these things, but I don't. Fact is, she'd rather I not talk to her at all. She wants to sit at the cool table at school, and having a brother like me isn't helping her cause. She avoids me like I carry the plague of unpopularity.

"Lets go inside," Robin says, then turns her back again to make another joke at my expense as this jury of twelve-year-olds judges me to be too strange. I say I don't care what anybody thinks of me. But deep down I know that's not true. If I really didn't care, then it wouldn't matter when they made fun of me. I would just let it bounce off me. Instead, I'm more like this grass: they cut me down, but I just grow back.

"Hey farm boy!" Alex yells from the Crown Vic when he pulls in the driveway just as I finish the lawn. I wipe the sweat from my brow and flick it his way. "You ready or what?"

"Change of plans," I shout over my shoulder as I return the mower to the tabernacle of tools. I don't bow to the Holy Camaro Being, but offer up a one-fingered salute before I shut the door.

"No Jellybean?" Alex sounds disappointed that our CD shop-a-thon might be off.

"I got big news," I say as I climb in, give him a friendly smack on the back, admire his new necklace of small silver skulls, and try not to burst his eardrum when I shout, "I'm in love."

As we drive to pick up Sean, then Kylee, I give Alex some details of the previous night. Alex doesn't ask a lot of questions, which is good because it's weird to talk about it. Stranger was that I didn't need to talk Kylee into it. We'd done standard make-out stuff from the first night, but things progressed in our few weeks together a lot faster than with Megan. Last night after ushering at

Whiting, I walked over to her house for a late dinner with her and her funny, funky parents, but Kylee had other plans, since they were out, and I was finally in.

"I'll never see you again," Alex finally says in a voice filled with mock hurt.

"Well, not as much as Kylee gets to see," I shoot back at him.

"Enough already!" Alex shouts. "One sex-filled night and you're already insufferable."

"No, I'm just done suffering," I reply as we pull up to Sean's huge two-story house.

Sean piles in, and I move to the backseat. We listen to demos of new Alex songs during the short trip to Kylee's house. Kylee lives over in the Cultural Center area, which houses the art museum, the library, and the Whiting. We'll pick her up, then head over to the Jellybean store down on Fenton Road. Jellybean is this great used CD, DVD, video, and book store that's our home away from home. I used to make my mom take me almost every Saturday when I was in eighth grade, blowing my whole allowance to buy some cool book I'd read about. Mom made up the difference between what I wanted and the money I needed to buy it. She never told my dad about these income supplements, since they were not earned old-school style. Now, Alex, Sean, and I are weekend regulars, even if Sean does most of the spending while Alex and I settle for window-shopping.

Kylee's sitting on the front step of her parent's house smoking a cigarette and letting the hot, bright sun bounce off her cool Ray-Bans. She's wearing a tight white T-shirt, denim cutoffs, and huge hoop earrings that I'm ready to jump through at her request. She doesn't just walk to the car; she dances toward us and I can't take my eyes off her, nor can Sean or Alex. She greets me with a kiss on the lips, while Alex gets a quick one on the hand rather than on his zit-filled face.

"Kylee, this is Sean," I say, bursting with pride.

"Nice outfit," she says after giving Sean's frat-boy wardrobe the once-over, then rolls her eyes. "So, are you a sailor with Old Navy, or what?"

Sean shoots that shy-guy smile first at Kylee, then at me. Before he can respond, she gives him a kiss on the cheek. "Just teasing, kid," she says as she climbs into the backseat.

"Wow, Bret, she's tenriffic," Sean says, grabbing my arm before I join Kylee in the back. As Alex pulls the Crown Vic back on the road, I feel for the first time like I belong after all on this human highway.

Five

Freak faggot."

I outwardly ignore all-American asshole Bob Hitchings's usual greeting as I take my seat, but the words beat me down inside. It's first period on the first day of my junior year in English class, the great melting pot that makes big fat fibbers out of our Founding Fathers. All men are not created equal; some are smarter, some are stronger. If Jefferson, Madison, and the rest of their ilk had spent a day at Southwestern, they would have flushed that claptrap right down the toilet. I'm smarter than a lot of people in this room, more talented in the things that matter to me. But guys like Hitchings, who are stronger than most people, and guys like me, who are smarter than most people, are not equals. A born athlete, Hitchings cares about kicking a football, capturing a wrestling-pin fall, and catching a baseball. I'm a born artist who cares about books, music, and theater. In my eyes, he isn't better than me, nor am I better than him; we're just different, and different is okay with me.

Mr. King starts junior English by announcing he'll be teaching a unit on poetry, well, trying to teach. Coach King, as the jockarchy calls him, or Mold King Cold as Alex, Sean, and I call him, is a good example of man's inequality to man. No way he and my drama teacher, Mr. Douglas, were created equal. Mr. D. lives to teach, to make us better, whereas Mr. King teaches so he can coach. Scholastics are a bother to him, sports is what matters. Mold King Cold fits right in at my school. People like King pass on the privileged and piss on the rest of us.

King tells us to choose a poem from the textbook to read aloud tomorrow. Almost everyone sighs, but he just laughs, noting that once we did this, we wouldn't have to touch poetry for the rest of the year. I raise my hand. "Mr. King, does it have to come from the text?"

"Coach King." The look he gives me is like a sniper taking a bead on his target. "What is your name, son?"

Before I can answer, one of the thickheads in the front mutters, "Freak boy."

It gets a laugh; King even seems to smile. I don't. I look down at my thrift store Dr. Evil watch: less than five minutes into my junior year and it has started again.

"Bret Hendricks," I answer, although I suspect he knows. He's just a dog lifting his leg.

"Hendricks." He grunts like my father when he says it.

"Do I get to ask my question?" I bellow over the laughter in the room. That sound doesn't bounce off me; it leaves little dents. Like Scottie says on those old *Star Trek* TV shows, "Captain, the shields can't take much more of this." Once the fall play starts, in a few weeks, I can recharge my batteries, but for now, I'm powerless. My fellow actors are my teammates: they give me support, even if we don't win letters or act as a closed clique. Water walkers like Hitchings are surrounded by people who prop them up, like it was a privilege.

"Make it quick, Hendricks." He sounds annoyed. Hell, he is annoyed.

"Does the poem have to be from the textbook?" More laughter, more annoyance. I sense a pattern developing. Eight more months of this to go, plus another year.

"Probably some homo poem." That came from behind me, from Hitchings, just loud enough for me to hear. I wonder who shaved his back each morning and taught him to walk upright. It was during my freshman year and my pathetic attempt to become a wrestler when Hitchings and his bunch first started riding me. They were all athletes, making the mat yet another place where I just didn't fit—but I didn't quit. Having no muscle mass, no killer instinct, and a total inability to grasp the world's oldest sport, which was nothing like the wrestling I watched on TV, I endured a three-month hell of getting my face rubbed into the stinky, popped-zit-infested wrestling mat. They'd be cranking on me, driving a chin into my shoulder or elbow into my groin, spitting into my ear, "You ain't shit, faggot." The abuse transferred from the mat to a daily dose of insults directed at both Alex, whom Hitchings calls Alexandra, and at me.

I had the unfortunate fate to fall next to Hitchings in the alphabet, which in elementary school helped us become friends. But since middle school, when he got heavy into sports, his father started making money and they moved from our neighborhood, we'd stopped hanging out. In any class we've shared in high school, he's bounced pencils off my neck, kicked the back of my desk, and called me names. He picks on Alex too, but he leaves Sean alone, since their dads are friends and they live in the same neighborhood. Sean keeps his distance from him to my relief.

nailed

"Can I read something I wrote instead of something from the text?" I ask over more laughter, determined this year I won't let jockarchy intimidate me into inane conformity.

"You just wanna do things the hard way, don't you, Hendricks?" King shoots back, then smiles. My father asked the same question, and like him, King didn't really want an answer, not that I owed him an explanation. A very long year just got longer.

The next morning I feel excited yet indecisive. I've got some of my own stuff I want to read, although none of it is as good as the poems and lyrics in Alex's jam-packed notebooks. But I don't want to waste it on the likes of Hitchings. I have plenty to choose from in my copy of *The Outlaw Book of Poetry*. I finally decide on reading the first part of Allen Ginsberg's *Howl*.

I never get the chance. King starts from the back of the room in the radical reverse alphabetical order. When he calls Hitchings's name, there is a low rumble of laughter.

"Coach, I would like to read a poem that I wrote," Bob Hitchings says to my stunned disbelief. I'm convinced he doesn't know or care about the difference between a couplet and a catcher's mitt.

"That would be fine, Bob," Mr. King responds.

Hitchings walks to the front of the gloomy room. He clears his throat, then starts:

Alex's a maggot, Bret's a faggot.
Call one freak, other little Bretty.
I wish they'd both freaking leave already.

Only Sean doesn't seem amused at my embarrassment as laughter fills the room.

"That's enough, Bob," King finally says; his tone suggests he's protecting, not correcting. Everybody acts like nothing out of the ordinary had occurred. "Your turn to read, Hendricks."

"Pass," is all I say, my face turning redder.

It gets worse. The next incident is a week later. I've become not the teacher's pet, but his bitch. King must be on Dad's payroll, working the school shift at the breaking-down-Bret factory.

King is going around the class asking his football followers about the upcoming Homecoming dance. Our band isn't invited to play, so I have no interest in going. When Kylee and I want to dance or otherwise entwine our bodies, we don't need any on-lookers or special occasion. I notice King's not talking to anyone else in the class, not to the girls, and certainly not to me.

"Hey, Mr. King, aren't you going to ask me who I'm taking to the dance?" I ask.

He grunts, which is fine. I have a scathing speech I have dreamed of making one day about the idiocy of school dances and athletics. I've just been waiting for an opening, and here it is.

"I didn't ask you," King says, walking over toward me. He leans into me, his wide arms pressing down on my desk, then winks at Hitchings. "I assume you're taking Alex Shelton."

It gets a big laugh from Hitchings and the other thick-necked brownnosers in earshot. The laugh gives me the second I need to do what I've never done before: fight back.

"No, I'm taking your wife," I shout, getting the attention of the whole room.

"That will earn you a day," he replies, quickly and sharply, then returns to his desk.

"Taking her all the way, know what I mean?" I add, no smile outside, a huge one inside.

"Make that two days." Twenty-five other people are in the room, but they no longer matter. This isn't about them; it's about turf. He lifts his leg on me, I'll piss on him right back.

"How about—" I start.

"Another word and we'll make it a week." He ends it by scribbling a note and reaching for the phone. "Go see Principal Morgan. I'm sure you know the way to his office."

King is right about one thing: I've clashed with Principal Robert Morgan many times in my less-than-crystal-clear two years at Southwestern. I took my time walking the Stephen King–like *Green Mile* to his office, listening to the sound of my footsteps in empty hallways filled with drab, tan lockers and drabber off-white cement walls. I walked by the school's sports trophy display case and started humming an old folk tune that Kylee's history professor father taught me, "If I Had a Hammer." I dream of one day smashing the case and hearing the sound of breaking glass as I shatter the jockarchy's shrine.

"Coach King phoned," Morgan says, his face looking like he'd just won a lemon-sucking contest, after I'm finally admitted to see His Harshness.

"Here," I hand him the pass, put my hat on, and slouch in the chair, my long legs dangling over the other chair, reserved no doubt for my father if this escalates any further.

"Lose the hat, smart guy," he says sharply, thereby convincing me that all school principals must be recruited from the military. "Sit up straight."

I salute him, but he doesn't get that I'm mocking him.

"When are you going to shape up, Hendricks?" Morgan asks me. He doesn't care about the answer. Like my dad, he just enjoys asking the question.

"Maybe I should become a jock, then I would get in shape," I shoot back.

"Lose that tone, smart guy." Attacking the jockarchy was attacking the status quo. Messing with it was messing with the bottom line. "I want you to see Mrs. Pfeil."

"Thank you, sir," I say. Sarcasm is lost on Morgan. Mrs. Pfeil is one of the school counselors. I have a hard time reconciling her ability to help students plan their college careers with talking us out of suicide. Maybe it was the same skill: focusing on the future. I know that game because thinking about busting out of high school, and away from Flint and my dad, is all that keeps me going some days.

"Maybe she can talk some sense into you," Morgan says, acting like he even cares.

"Maybe." I give him an overly dramatic shoulder shrug.

"She had better. Someone has to get through to you." His eyes turn away from me, the papers on his desk are more interesting, important, and urgent than me, apparently. "One more incident like this, and it is between me and your father. Is that what you want? Two more and school policy is that you are out of this school. Do you understand what I'm saying to you?"

"Whatever." I won't play this game, namely because all I can do is lose.

"Do your parents know that you dress like this?" Morgan has two suits: the dark blue one and the very dark blue one and an endless supply of plain white shirts and bland striped ties.

"It's okay with them." If sarcasm is lost on him, I wonder about the truth. Every time I add tint to my hair, I blow a colorful cruel wind into my dad's black-and-white world.

"If the school board's lawyer, Mr. Walker, would let us have a stricter dress code or uniforms, then you would be lost, buster." Morgan had a way of talking sometimes that seemed like he was reading off cue cards. I think in his perfect world, he'd just slap us all around and make us drop and give him twenty push-ups. Old school.

"Maybe I should wear blue suits and striped ties every day then." That one flew right over his crew cut.

"Disrespecting teachers will not be tolerated. Your behavior is totally unacceptable," Morgan says, handing me the official suspension paperwork, which neither Mom nor I would let my dad see, knowing his reprimand would become even more relentless.

"You're right; it is unacceptable for King to talk to me like that," I say, hat off, but spine still lazily bent, even though it was about time I showed a little for once in my life.

"What?" His eyes are busting so far out of his head that he looks like a frog.

"Mr. King hassles me," I say, this confession and confrontation building for two years.

"That's not true, you know that." Morgan was trying to get rid of me. Eye contact was on the downslide, irritating sighs were on the increase. "Coach King is a fine man, a great teacher, and an asset to this school."

"He's an asset, all right," I say, fighting back the urge to use a different word. Morgan stares at me, and the look of his furrowed caveman brow reflects the Neanderthal tone of school. It wasn't just Hitchings, it was the whole hostile environment. It was getting pushed in the hallway and having books knocked out of my hands. It was getting called names. It was all of these things. It was everything. And it was me.

"Have you ever thought, Mr. Hendricks, that if you didn't act or dress so oddly things would be easier for you?" Morgan says, playing pin the tail on the victim.

"You're right, it's my fault," I say, unable to rein in my sarcasm in this shit storm.

"Just keep up with the smart remarks like that, and you'll spend a lot of time in here," Morgan says, confident in his ability to predict my future.

"Maybe," I mumble, wondering if there's any way I can ever win.

Morgan opens up a folder and pulls out a piece of paper. "What's your father's phone number at work?" he asks. "It's not listed here."

"Call my mom. She's at home," I reply, dodging the question.

"Wait outside," he says after a long sigh.

As I get up to leave the office, I know that I'm not just odd: I must be crazy. It's insane to keep doing the same things and expect different results. I cram the suspension slip into my pocket, tucking it deep using only an extended, if hidden, middle finger. As I exit Morgan's office to wait for my mother in the safer outer sanctum, I consider cracking my thick head hard into Morgan's concrete wall, giving action to the agony of my hopelessness and madness.

Six

I don't think I can take it anymore, Mom."

"I know it's rough for you, Bret," my mom says, muting the always-blaring TV.

"It's too hard," I say through clenched teeth, anger directed inward at my impotent indecision. I don't want to be a victim, but I'm clueless as to how to be the victor.

She nods, then sits down next to me on the dingy sofa in our Value City–decorated living room. Our house is cluttered, and often unclean, since Mom is too busy working, I don't have time, and Robin doesn't care about anything except herself, her room, and her girlfriends.

"I hate those bastards at school. I hate them! Is that wrong?" I make sure to first look to see that Robin isn't around before I let loose with words not fit for twelve-year-old ears.

"No, Bret, I don't think that's wrong. I think it's natural, but—"

"But what?"

"You can't sink to their level," my mom says, clueless about the whole truth. I told her about the taunts but lacked the nerve to mention my lack of courage as I let Hitchings assault me in King's class. I knew better than to fight Hitchings, knowing I would lose the battle and the war. Sticks and stones harmed me, but not as bad as the humiliation of his hammering me down.

"And why not?" I respond.

"Because you're better than that," she reassures me, even as almost daily my dad destroyed my confidence, while my mom built it back up. They were working at cross-purposes, which made as much sense as anything else in their strained and strange marriage.

"That's corny."

"Do you trust me, Bret?" Her hand is trembling a tiny bit. I noticed that when she got nervous, or upset, her hand would twitch, like she was trying to shake out the stress.

"Sure, Mom." She protected me from my dad. How could I not trust her?

"When people put you down, it's to build themselves up," she says, stroking my hair, not caring about the color and length. She dislikes talk about personal appearances, since like many people in Flint, she and Dad are overweight, out of shape, and owners of several XL outfits.

"Well, they're pretty tall then," I say, trying to make a joke.

"Only if you make them," she says in all seriousness. "Just consider the source."

"What?"

"Consider the source. These people who make fun of you, do you like them or even respect them?"

"No, they're ass—"

"Assholes. It's okay, Bret. That's what they sound like." I think it's the first time I've ever heard her curse. She's real religious, punching her church time clock every Sunday. She prays for me, but I gave up on God long before Hitchings started bedeviling me.

"Mom, do I need to get soap for your mouth?" I joke, although I wouldn't put that type of punishment past my father. For the first eight years of my life, he mainly preferred his belt. For the past eight, he takes away the attention and consideration scraps he throws my way.

"So what they say doesn't make any difference," she says, although I doubt she'd been through anything like this as a teenager. My mom is so damn normal it is almost strange.

"I guess . . ."

"It only matters what you think about yourself."

"In that case . . . ," I say with a hint of sarcasm, slumping farther down into the sofa, wishing it would swallow me up and spit me back out as normal as Mom was and Dad wanted me to be.

"Bret, I'm sorry that I don't have any other words of wisdom for you. I just want you to be happy," my mom says. It's her constant refrain. As I look around the living room, it was obvious that in my house *happy* equaled entertainment with my sister's Anime DVDs, my old professional wrestling videos, and Mom's piles of used paperback romance novels stacked everywhere. Dad kept his entertainment in the garage and thoughts on happiness to himself.

"Well that's part of the problem, Mom," I reply.

"What do you mean?" Unlike my father, when my mom asked a question, she actually wanted to hear the answer.

"I think while you're trying to make sure I'm happy, Dad is trying to make sure that I'm miserable."

"Your father loves you, Bret. You know that, don't you?" she says, although the frown on her face contradicts her.

"No, I don't."

"You're too hard on your father," Mom says, that voice so

warm while explaining away my father's coldness. "He just doesn't understand you, your music, how you dress. One day you'll have children of your own and—"

"I don't think so, but if I do, I know I'll be a better father to them than he is to me."

My mother didn't say anything. I was putting her in the middle, and that wasn't fair, but maybe her silence said more than any words. Silence was welcome, since it seemed once or twice a week, the house was full of anything but. They would yell, then my father would slam a door and retreat into the garage to work on his vintage Camaro, driving off into his past. I never asked, nor did I need to, because I had the timing figured out. I knew every fight was about me.

"You have to appreciate your father. He's a good man who has had a hard life."

"Well, I guess that makes it right."

"I'm not excusing how your father treats you sometimes, Bret, I'm trying to explain it," my mother says. "He wants the world for you; he just has a hard time expressing himself."

"I don't think so," I reply.

"Really, he wants a better life for you, better than he has," she continues. "Trust me, he didn't wake up one morning and decide he wanted to manage a car wash for a living."

"What did he want to do after college?" My dad never talked about work in front of me. I only knew this was his latest job, his third dirty one since I'd been in high school. He was out of work a lot when I was younger. I learned later that since we didn't have any health insurance, my ear operations and other health problems got us into deep debt.

"When your father and I were growing up, we didn't think

about things like that. We never thought about college after high school."

"Why was that?" I asked, even though I knew the answer as well as I knew the sound of my mother's expansive sigh.

"Bret, don't act so coy. You're good in math. Add it up." I hide my smile. Like my dad's weekly Monday night AA meetings, my parent's history was one of the many unspoken subjects in our house. My mom just turned forty. My parents had been married twenty-two years, and my brother, Cameron, was twenty-three.

"But what about later?" Trying to figure out my parent's life was my real homework.

"It just wasn't in the cards." I wonder who she is trying to convince, me or herself, that their lives rested more on a matter of fate than fateful choices. "Then you came along, and soon after your father got laid off from the factory and needed to find work. It wasn't meant to be."

"You're too easy on him, Mom."

"And I think you're too hard on him, and on yourself. He's a good man, a good husband, a good provider, and he's a good person battling every day to remain one, but . . ."

"A big-ass but."

"He's not perfect, he's just a person."

"So why is he so hard on me?"

"We're doing the best we can," she says, wrapping her arms around me and pulling me close. "I wish we could have a bigger house and some money in the bank. I wish that your father could find a better job and so does he. I wish that Cam could get a better job too. I wish we had money to send you and Robin to private schools. I wish for lots of things."

"So do I, Mom, so do I." I laugh, but she just frowns.

"There's a big difference between wishes at sixteen and wishes once you're past forty."

"Why, what's a wish once you're past forty?" I ask, falling for her trap.

"A regret," she says, getting up to go wash greasy dishes, having temporarily cleaned up all of my troubles. As she leaves the room, I realize that she has somehow pulled all that pain from out of my body and put it into hers. My mother is the perfect empathy machine.

Seven

You're either part of the problem or—"

"Part of the solution," Kylee's mom says, finishing her husband's sentence. Their constant dinner table chatter, talking over each other and Kylee, is as strange to me as the Thai food we're finishing off.

"You need to stand up for yourself, and others, and denounce this intolerance," Kylee's father declares, his voice booming. I'd been telling them over dinner about Hitchings and my suspension for talking back to King. While my mother offered only empathy and my father remained ignorant, Kylee's parents were in solution mode, much to Kylee's annoyance.

"Why don't you run for Student Council and make a speech about your feelings?" Mrs. Edmonds asks, but Kylee seems both embarrassed and irritated by her parents' interest in me.

"I don't think so," I reply, getting a hand squeeze show of support from Kylee. "I mean that's like so ordinary. I'll leave that to the Becca Levys of the world."

"Who's Becca?" Kylee asks.

"She's one of these involved-in-everything types," I tell her, leaving out both Becca's "mental babe" comment, as well as my unstated interest in her, normal or not. Besides, standing up in front of the school and spleen venting against daily nightmares is just a daydream. It is one thing to act onstage, it is another to take part in a public verbal action against Hitchings.

"You need to do something. History teaches us that the worst thing for good people to do is nothing," Mr. Edmonds tells me as he gets up from the table. "Like the sit-down strike."

"The what?" I reply, dumb to any history not involving music or movies.

"The Great Flint Sit-Down Strike," Kylee whispers, rushing to my rescue. "That's his favorite class that he teaches at U of M–Flint. Don't get him started or they'll never leave."

"Right, the Sit-Down Strike here in Flint," I say, punching the words with confidence.

"I don't believe they don't teach you about these things in school," he says, annoyed, yet his smile never wavers. "I'll give you some books to read on it, Bret."

I stifle a laugh: he wants to give me books; my dad wants me to work more, read less. Mr. Edmonds retreats toward the book-filled living room, while Mrs. Edmonds checks her cell for messages. He returns with a copy of *Sit-Down* by Sidney Fine and puts it in my left hand.

"Mom, don't you need to be going?" Kylee says, sarcasm dripping rich and thick.

"How do I look?" her mom asks us, but I'm stumped knowing if I should answer. She's a slightly larger, older version of Kylee, although dressed for success not for dancing.

"Like Robin Hood," Kylee replies. Her mom heads toward the door, where her dad helps her put on her coat. My father's appearance reflected his bad habits of smoking and starchy foods, while Kylee's dad resembles a hobbit; short, sturdy, and slightly round.

"Robin Hood?" I whisper.

"They're going to yet another fund-raiser," Kylee says softly. "Mom guilts the rich into giving to the poor or the library or the museum or whomever she's working for. Right now, she's working for the North End Food Bank."

"I thought she was an artist," I say, since the evening had started with Mrs. Edmonds showing me some of her paintings.

"Artist, writer, fund-raiser, professor's wife, community leader, and socialite," Kylee says. "She doesn't have jobs, she has crusades. Didn't you know my mom is Wonder Woman?"

I laugh loudly, but get it together to wave good-bye to her parents as they exit. "I really like having dinner and hanging with your parents, Kylee," I say once they are out the door. I set down the *Sit-Down* book on the table, unsure when I'll have time to read the massive tome.

"Do you want them?" Kylee asks, then shakes her head.

"No, thanks. I got my hands full with my own," I reply. As much as I like her parents, I don't know if I could handle them on a daily basis. The main thing I could tell was that while Kylee might be their only child and center of attention, it was hard for her, or me, to get a word in edgewise in the Edmonds house.

"It's all about them and their achievements," Kylee says, as she picks up the last spring roll with chopsticks, taking a bite and feeding the rest to me. "My parents have done and seen everything, so what's left for me?"

"Kylee, don't be silly," I reassure her. Kylee loved to dance at other people's parties, but she delighted in throwing herself a pity party, not that I understood why. I couldn't imagine someone as beautiful, talented, and loved as Kylee having a worry in the world. Maybe everybody else's life—even Sean's—isn't as perfect as it appears when you are on the outside looking in.

"You know what I call my mother in my journal?" she asks, knowing full well I have no idea and that I long for a sneak peak into her secret life. Kylee might let me in between her sheets, but she would never let me read between those purple covers. Her journal was under lock and key in her antique-looking rolltop desk, and no combination of hints or heavy breathing would allow me a taste of that forbidden fruit. "I call my lovely mother 'the ShadowCaster.'"

"Sounds like a villain in a video game, not a superhero," I joke, but Kylee isn't laughing.

"I wouldn't know about that," she says. She is, per parental decree, a video game virgin.

"Well, we're able to enjoy other forms of physical entertainment," I say, pulling my chair closer to her and away from the Thai food left from dinner.

"Well, that entertainment is fun, free, and quite fulfilling."

"Kylee, please." My face turns red, my regular reaction to Kylee's obvious advances.

"Are you embarrassed, cutie?"

"No, it's just—" I stop short, not sure how to explain my feelings.

"Despite what some jealous types might tell you, I'm not a skank or anything," Kylee says, putting her head against my chest.

"I never thought—" I start.

"Unlike a lot of girls, I don't get drunk and sleep around. I sleep with who I want, when I want," Kylee says, pulling at her short black skirt. "And you, Bret Hendricks, are what I want."

"I feel the same," I say, pulling her closer, connecting her skin with mine.

"It's like dancing. When I find someone I want to be with, then why not? Why be alone?"

The beating of my heart, the racing of my pulse, and the lump in my jeans speak for me.

"I guess that makes me different, but that's okay. You like different, right?" she asks, answering her own question. "It's not that big of a deal for me. It's not like some sort of crusade. It's just who I am. If people don't like me, then that's their problem, not mine."

"You don't catch any shit at school for this look?" I ask, stroking her violet hair.

"Maybe it's just Central or because I'm a woman or a senior, but no, it's not a big deal with me or my friends," she explains, as I dream of a school where being the exception ruled.

"And your parents?"

"Please," she says, stretching out the vowels in time with an exaggerated eye roll.

"They're just so different from my parents," I say, stating the obvious. Kylee's parents aren't just different from my folks, but from anybody's parents I'd ever met. The Edmondses treat me like a real person, not a freak boy. While tonight my mom is clerking for Wal-Mart and my dad's doing a classic car street cruise, her folks are at some event raising funds to feed and shelter the homeless. That fit, because Mr. and Mrs. Edmonds did a great job of making me feel at home in their house.

"They're different, all right," Kylee says, as she clears the cartons of Thai food from the table. This is a perfect example: I'd never had Thai food in my house in my life. Kylee and her parents wielded chopsticks with the same skill that Sean worked his drumsticks, while I fought with even using a fork. The weirdest thing is how I felt different, but not out of place. I always knew that I wasn't a typical high school misfit, it was just that I hadn't hit on my fit yet. I'm more of a stranger in my own house, than here.

"What do you want to do now?" I ask, getting off my exhausted ass to help. While I treasure theater, love singing in my band, and long for alone time with Kylee, I can't believe how hard it is to keep all the plates spinning, even for someone with as much energy as me.

"Silly, silly man," Kylee says with a wink, motioning me toward her in the kitchen. Not that I need the encouragement. "I thought we could nudge-nudge, wink-wink."

"Not that again!" I say to my sarcastic sweetie.

She pushes out her plumlicious bottom lip in a pretend pout, which I suck on with pleasure. With Megan, sex was like a game of strip poker. At each encounter, I'd ante up and she'd surrender another layer of clothing. Kylee isn't nearly as shy about showing her body or sharing it with me, although now that we are a couple, I wish she would show it off a little less, maybe wear looser and longer clothes.

"Read the shirt," Kylee says, pointing at her bright tight red T-shirt with a picture of a woman named Emma Goldman proclaiming, "If I can't dance, I don't want to be part of your revolution." She makes it easier to read by tugging on my ponytail and pulling me closer.

"Let's dance then," I say, as we make our way into the living room. The Edmonds's house is filled with books and magazines hidden under a blanket of fallen feline fur. With five cats, my allergies are full blown, but I'm breathing in Kylee alone, she's my new oxygen. Thankfully, her bedroom is normally cat- and clutter-free, except for her cool collectibles.

Kylee is, as usual, a step ahead of me, already cuing up the music, some generic hip-hop. But there's nothing standard about Kylee's dancing, which mixes years of classical ballet with the best moves seen on BET. As we dance, she rubs against me and I'm lost in a fever. During the summer, when she would be talking with me, she would sometimes put her hand on my arm, almost sending me into shock, as if electricity were running through my body. Now, after dancing up a sweat, we waltz toward the shower to wash it off.

We take a long shower, extended by my sincere attempt to cover every single one of her sixty inches with either soapy caresses or sweet kisses. We emerge into a bathroom deep in steam. Kylee hands me a thick white towel, while I watch the thin beads of water cascade down her body. The steam is making this night seem unreal, like most of my almost two months with Kylee. Though I had imagined it, I never knew if I could connect with anyone like this. I want to believe that Kylee is the cure for all that ails me.

"Is something wrong?" Kylee asks, noticing that I'm lost in thought.

"I want to know something," I say, steam filling my lungs and doubt clouding my eyes. I need to know this is real. From my father to Megan the Imposter to the jockarchy, I've been dealing with a load of rejection, so standing naked with Kylee in front of the steamed-up mirror, our images barely reflecting back, I need to understand where we stand with each other.

She silences my words with a kiss, then moves in front of me, her back pressed up against my front. I bury my thoughts and then my face in the nape of Kylee's neck, where her white skin explodes into a plume of violet hair. I savor every second, as I suck up the sexiness of her body and the sensations it arouses in me.

"Look up," Kylee whispers. I glance up to see written words on the steamy mirror: "Kylee loves Bret." I've been thinking, feeling, and wanting to say those words, but Kylee seizes them for herself and steals my breath away.

Megan the Imposter said she loved me too, but I never believed her. I'd heard her lie to her parents and to herself about who she really was. Her love was another pose, a false promise, and playing pretend. Megan couldn't have been mine because she didn't even belong to herself.

Kylee takes my hand and leads me toward her bedroom; my happiness is about making her happy. Meanwhile in the bathroom, I imagine that the heat is fading, the cold air entering, and the steam disappearing from the mirror, taking with it the message, "Kylee loves Bret." As I stroke my all-thumbs fingers along her graceful dancer thighs, I take time on my knees to pray that even when those three words vanish, the feeling never will.

Eight

Welcome to Radio-Free Flint!"

With those words, Radio-Free Flint debuts in the parking lot of Southwestern High School on the night of the Homecoming dance on a perfectly crisp fall Michigan evening. We ripped off the name from Flint's hometown antihero Michael Moore. I hope he doesn't sue us, because we don't have any money, my dad hates lawyers, and it's the only name all three of us band mates liked.

Alex, Sean, and I had spent most of the past week rehearsing in Sean's basement. It was really the only choice, since Alex and his mom live in a small apartment. There was also no way we could have rehearsed at my house, since it would've meant changing the chorus of every song to incorporate my father yelling, "Turn that racket down!" Besides, God forbid our rehearsals interfere with something important, like waxing the Camaro for the thousandth time.

I don't get that about Dad. Even though I hate everything about his obsession with that damn car, I half admire that he cares about *something* so much. If he's so damn passionate about an ordinary thing, why can't he understand how much I care about my band?

The band has played a couple times at small parties some of the theater folks hosted, but this night is our official debut. Of course, we'd hoped it would have been inside the school, not in the littered parking lot. Sadly, Will Kennedy, Becca Levy, and the rest of the Homecoming committee hired a DJ, a mere spinner of CDs, and told us that our funk-punk wasn't needed.

So we're having our concert on the concrete, between the yellow lines. This will literally give us street credibility. We aren't full-blown punks or real rappers, but we share their attitude; outside, looking in suits us perfectly. Our sound is a blistering blend of Sean's and my punked-up funk rhythms, Alex's machine-gun heavy-treble guitar, and my shout-and-sing vocal style.

We borrowed my dad's purchased-for-an-emergency generator. Well, "borrowed" might imply that I asked permission and he agreed, so I guess "stole with the intention of returning" is a more accurate description. We shoved it in the back of the Crown Vic, which has a trunk that could sleep twenty, and set it up while everyone was at the football game. We used Alex's car and Sean's silver SUV as curtains to hide the gear.

As the Southwestern student sheep move toward the gym, Sean starts thumping the big bass drum to create a thundercloud of rhythm raining over students and proud alumni just across the circle driveway.

Once we reach a critical mass, Alex and I slowly back up his car and Sean's SUV to "open the curtain" on our little makeshift stage. We turn the cars at just such an angle so the headlights act as our spotlights. We cut the engines, and then bound out of the cars. Alex plugs in the Gibson, creating a wailing wall of screeching feedback that sounds more beautiful to me than anything on earth. I strap on my bass, then clutch the microphone like my life depends on it, and in a way, it does. I have imagined this moment for years. I wink at Kylee, who's wildly adorned in a skin-tight blood red dress, then leave the fringes for center stage.

We fire off with Alex's best song ("Matter of Fact"). Alex and I fought about the set list until he came to pick me up. He wanted to only do his songs, but I fought for one classic cover because for all my "don't give a crap" complaining, I really want everybody to like us.

Except for that, Alex and I disagree on very little, about the band or anything else. We are not soul mates or fraternal twins sent to different homes, but rather Siamese twins separated at birth, once joined at the head. We must have shared one brain for a few years, since we think alike on just about everything except the merits of cover versions.

For the debut, we decide we'll do all his material, but we'll end with a cover of "London Calling" by The Clash, a song older than me that's still played on Ann Arbor alternative radio. We'll change the title to "Burton Calling" to poke fun at Flint's feeble eastside suburb. Alex's angry opus ("Throw the Lions to the Christians") about water walkers like Hitchings will be the encore.

We never get that far. It is not long into our set before one very angry führer Robert D. Morgan comes upon the scene in all his blue-suited and red-faced glory.

I signal to Alex and Sean to just keep playing. I know if there is a sound of silence, Morgan would loudly fill it.

"You are creating a disturbance!" Morgan shouts, putting his hand over the microphone. "You are not authorized to do this!"

"We wanted to play inside, but they wouldn't let us," I yell at him as Alex cranks up the volume on the amps. Morgan just looks at me. He's used to deference, not defiance.

"You are not allowed to do this!" he repeats to me, close enough for me to enjoy the moist mix of his spit with my sweat.

I turn my back on Morgan and we keep playing. Morgan might own the school in the day, but tonight, his students and his parking lot belong to us. We have gathered quite a crowd, and they've not been standing still. They've been moving to the music, with Kylee and some of her girlfriends from Central up front and leading the way. Kylee would periodically stop spinning like a red top long enough to capture images of the band with Sean's digital camera. On this one night, I have never felt so free or powerful, so it's no wonder I'm not afraid of Morgan.

Before we launch into our next song, Alex's epic ass-kicker, "Trinkets," we lose our power, literally. Morgan's security stooges have shut the generator down. "I'll see you three on Monday," are his departing words to us, very cool, very in control.

I never acknowledge him. He is nothing to me. I've pulled back the curtain of fear.

"May I have your attention!" I shout, crawling on the hood of Alex's Crown Vic. "We'll do the rest of the set tonight in the parking lot of Kmart at ten thirty."

"That was great. We should have had you guys play inside," Becca Levy says to us as she and a bunch of her not-so-geeky popular-crowd girlfriends applaud wildly.

"That was cool with Morgonzo," Will Kennedy says; he's this strange half-jock and half-jazz-band creature. It's clear many of my fellow Spartans liked our clash with Morgan.

I shake a few hands, but sadly no autographs are requested. I take the Fedora off, wipe the sweat off my forehead, pull the rubber band from my hair, letting the ponytail explode and my hair cover my damp shoulders. Kylee comes up, giving each of us a big hug, and then embarrasses me with a huge public kiss, which I think was for Becca's benefit, not mine.

"Kmart on Miller Road, right?" Will asks, and I answer him with a high five.

"Let's get going," I say, my passion for the moment far too obvious.

"I gotta break this stuff down," Sean whines, although I detect more of a whiskey odor.

"What's the rush?" Alex asks as he tucks the Gibson into its case. "We got time."

"We have an errand," I say, picking up Sean's cymbals and putting them in his SUV.

"What's up?" Alex asks.

"We're gonna send Morgan a little reminder." My face is almost fluorescent. "We'll take Alex's car, get the goods, and Sean and Kylee, why don't you just meet us there."

"Where is there?" Sean asks.

I'm halfway into Alex's car when I shout back, "The Rock."

The Rock is a Flint tradition. Located down the street from Southwestern, it is a small concrete structure that houses water pumps, or something like that. It doesn't matter what is on the inside, because only the outside matters; it is a canvas for every celebration or cause. There has to be a thousand coats of paint on it. We'll be one-thousand-and-one. This might be Homecoming, but I'm not coming home; instead, I feel like I'm starting to come into my own.

After a quick run to a hardware store off Fenton Road, we have an ample supply of white and black paint, plus brushes and two flashlights. Sean is sitting on top of the Rock when Alex and I get back, while Kylee is in the car writing in her ever-present journal.

I hand her the set list, which she tucks away inside the purple binder as a keepsake. It takes the three of us less than an hour, which will give us enough time to get over to the Kmart parking lot for our encore set.

We sit on top of the Rock, watching the cars exiting early from the Homecoming dance. When their headlights shine on the Rock, the stark white background reflecting and pushing out the thick black letters, they'll get the message. I just know this is the way that Morgan drives home to his cozy suburban castle in Grand Blanc. We have the last four words in black block letters, each one almost two feet high, loud and proud enough for Morgan, Hitchings, and his fellow gridiron goons, and all the gods and goddesses of Southwestern High to see:

RADIO-FREE
FLINT FOREVER

Nine

Was it worth it? Gimme a hell yes!"

Alex agrees, clinking his Vernor's ginger ale bottle against mine as we toast our Kmart musical conquest and Morgan clash of the night before. Not only did our contraband concert get us uninvited to school, which is more vacation than punishment, it also got us invited to Will Kennedy's house for a party, where some people who once scorned us now celebrate our success.

"Where's Sean?" I ask Alex because we're both worried about him. He's upset about the suspension, plus he just got dumped by his latest squeeze.

Kylee emerges from the basement, talking with Will and his friend-but-not-girlfriend Becca. Kylee's no doubt been dancing downstairs; her violet hair is damp, and she probably doesn't realize she's just a few drops of sweat on her tight white tank top from winning a wet T-shirt contest.

"Great party, Will!" Kylee says, giving him a quick hug, oblivious to his embarrassment.

"Thanks for coming, guys," Will replies. "Bret, if you ever need a backup drummer—"

"Sure thing!" Alex cuts him off and down with a sarcastic smile, which Will misses as he heads toward the door to greet more guests. I notice Kylee watches him walk away.

"I hate that guy," Alex says once Will is out of earshot.

"He seems cool enough," Kylee says sharply. "What's wrong with him?"

"Just look at him," I answer. "He doesn't know who he is: half jock, half jazz, and—"

"All jerk. The only letters he knows are the ones on his jacket," Alex declares.

Kylee frowns. "Alex, relax, you don't need to prove you're cool to me; I get it."

"I'm going to go find Sean," Alex says, no doubt biting his tongue. I feel like I'm playing a game of monkey in the middle as Alex and Kylee fight for my time and attention.

"He was downstairs playing DJ while I danced," Kylee says.

"Downstairs," Alex repeats, makes a drinking motion, and then walks away.

"Alex doesn't like me, you think?" Kylee says as we move outside to the porch where the smokers are gathering and grinding to techno music to fight off the evening chill.

"That's just Alex. You'll get used to him," I say, then collapse into an empty chair.

"Like your dad did, right?" Kylee replies as she starts moving to the music. As she sways, putting all the helpless dancers to shame, I'm overcome by how free she is in front of others and in her own home. Her parents treat Kylee and me like adults, not little kids. They know what's going on in their daughter's bedroom, yet according to Kylee, they say nothing. Her parents are hands-off about my putting hands on their daughter, letting her do just about whatever she wants, like some weird opposite world of the harshly ruled Hendricks household.

Since Kylee's never been any farther into my house than the driveway, she's yet to meet my parents, which is fine by me, although Mom says she wants to meet her. One day soon, I'll need to teach Kylee a lesson in Hendricks Family History 101: the men drink (although my father is sixteen years sober) and work dead-end jobs. I don't desire to do the dirty work my brother and father and grandfather before have done, from hanging drywall to working in car washes to getting splinters at a lumberyard, or any other work that breaks the soul and back at the same stupefying speed. I don't plan to live and die every day in Flint like them.

"What's with Sean tonight?" Kylee asks as she finally dances back over next to me.

"He said he broke up with his girlfriend," I say, choosing to ignore his occasional alcoholic overindulgences that convert him from shy-but-self-confident Sean into some asshole alter ego.

"Too bad for that sweet kid," Kylee says. She likes calling all of us kids since we're all juniors and she's a senior. "Sean's a good-looking guy; he'll get somebody else."

"I guess." I squirm in my seat, wondering why it's OK for Sean to ticket Kylee as tenriffic all the time, but her making comments about him churns up my envy engine.

"What's his story, anyway?" Kylee asks as she sits down on my lap.

I pull her closer. "What do you mean?"

"I mean other than hanging with us, he seems like just another future frat boy."

"You'd have to ask Alex; he's closer with Sean than I am,"

I say, unsure why I'm so uninterested in sharing what I do know about Sean's divided life with her. Two sets of parents and two sets of influences: the Lexus and Rolex bunch he's born into, and the Radio-Free Flint faction into which he fittingly belongs, not to mention his Dr. Jekyll/Mr. Jack Daniels duo.

"He's like us, hating all the pathetic posers out there," Kylee says, her confidence in her opinions total, especially when I nod in agreement. "Overall, I'd say that Sean's pretty cool."

"Maybe," I say with a shrug. I won't tell Kylee, but I know Sean finds his fellow mall-shopping SUV-driving set a bore, with their ideas and opinions stamped out like another GM assembly-line part. He can't bring himself to reject the trappings of his parents' privileged life, but he can't bring himself to embrace the mainstream. Like me, Sean admires Alex's in-your-face existence, but Sean doesn't want to deal with the bullyboys, like Hitchings from his block, who have started to arrive at the party and invade the back porch.

"Hey, dance with me," Kylee says, leaping up and then extending her arms.

"K, I'm exhausted," I say, producing on her bottom lip a pout of pure beauty, which overwhelms my chores in the morning, band practice in the day, and ushering at night weariness.

"Let's show these lug nuts what a real dancer looks like," Kylee says, then starts spinning small circles again on the porch, while some of Will's baseball buddies giggle at us.

"What are you looking at?" I say to the group while looking at the ground.

"What do you think?" Jack Bison, one of Hitchings's closest cronies cracks.

"Let's blow," I tell Kylee, but she's still dancing for her pleasure and my enemies' benefit. She's showing off, and showing them that, unlike me, she's resistant to their ridicule.

"She can stay Hendricks, but you're welcome to leave anytime," Bison says. I put my hand in my pocket and flip him off, but say nothing, since outwitting Bison would be child's play.

"That faggot wouldn't know what to do with a hot chick like that, anyway," Hitchings's voice booms behind me. He's standing in the doorway between the porch and the house.

"Come on, Kylee, let's go," I say, clutching her hand tightly.

"She's fine," Hitchings slurs.

I'm frozen in the heat of the moment. The only way out is through the door that Hitchings blocks with his massive frame. I'm trying to figure out what to do to get by Hitchings without humiliating myself in front of Kylee. I'm frozen in space and time when I notice Sean whisper something to Hitchings, who grunts, then steps away. Sean motions for us to join him, so Kylee and I slip by Hitchings, who manages to give me a slight shove. As I balance myself, Hitchings laughs loudly and then points his nose toward the sky. "I smell chickenshit."

As Kylee and I cross the threshold, I know he's just a creep. But he's also correct.

Ten

Bret, come on inside."

I enter school counselor Mrs. Pfeil's office without much enthusiasm. It's my first day back in school after Morgan's four-day suspension, although Sean somehow talked his way out of it, no doubt using skills taught to him by his lawyer parents. It is my second suspension and our school has a three-strike policy. I'm one more screwup away from kissing my career at Southwestern good-bye. I'll be shipped to an alternative school, where Flint's future felons, freebasers, and other losers labor their way toward a GED. As much as I hate it sometimes, I don't want to leave Southwestern, Alex, or Sean behind.

"What do you want to talk about today, Bret?" she asks. Unlike Morgan, she seems to really want to help me, but I'm beginning to think I'm hopeless.

"Let's talk about why Morgan hates me."

"Well, Bret, Mr. Morgan seems to think you have a problem with authority."

"Well, it's like Stone Cold Steve Austin used to say: 'I don't have a problem with authority because I am the authority!'" I do the Stone Cold salute, arms raised, although I leave out the up-turned middle finger. Mrs. Pfeil laughs at the performance.

nailed

"You'll have to help me here, Bret, who or what is 'Stone Cold'?"

Professional wrestling is my not-so-secret passion. Even though I don't really like sports, I appreciate the athletic effort that goes into wrestling, whether it's real or not. Add cool, larger-than-life characters, some great storytelling, and the drama inherent in banging a steel chair across someone's head, and you have almost everything I like rolled into one total package.

"Tell me about Stone Cold," Mrs. Pfeil says. Her pearl necklace suggests she's probably more a fan of theater-in-the-round than the squared circle. She's all business-suit style, but my rough rags don't bother her.

"He's a pro wrestler. His real name is Steve Williams," I explain, excited that someone is at least pretending to be interested. My father hates what he calls "rasslin'," and my mother rolls her eyes and leaves the room. Even Alex parts ways with me on this one. When the band formed, I told them Monday nights were off-limits for rehearsing because I needed to be in front of the TV watching the WWE's *Monday Night Raw* show. Not even Kylee can rip me away, and I've never had any luck trying to get her to watch what she calls "beefcake ballet."

"What do you like about him?" Mrs. Pfeil asks, like a straight man feeding me lines.

"Austin was the toughest SOB in the WWE," I say, echoing the phrase I heard every Monday night for years. "He's the kick-ass good guy who gets the last laugh."

"But Bret, isn't all of that fake?" She asks the unavoidable question.

"August 1997, Summer Slam. I own the video, and I've watched the match against Owen Hart at least ten times. Austin gets dropped on his head accidentally when Hart screws up a move called a pile driver. Austin is lying in the ring, not moving. Yet, he somehow manages to finish. He sits on the shelf and is told never to wrestle again. But Austin doesn't listen to anyone, except his own head and heart. Not wrestle? You might as well call the priest to say a few choice words in Latin. Stick a fork in him, he's done. But wait—he pulls the fork out! Not only that, he comes back, tough as ever!" I tell her, words falling over each other.

"You seem to admire this character," she says softly, then fills the room with silence.

"When Austin's music hit, when you heard that sound of glass breaking, he walked in and owned the place. He never backed down, he always got up when knocked down, and he always beat up the bad guys."

"That's very interesting," Mrs. Pfeil interjects.

"Really?" I'm unsure what she is getting at but eager to open up to someone. My father is impossible, and while my mom listens, and supplies sympathy, there's no real understanding. Mom lives her life in the soft, safe center of a Wal-Mart world. This is the kind of real conversation that I might have with Kylee's parents and long for with my own.

"Let's talk about someone closer to home. Your brother went to school here. He dropped out I recall. What's he like?" she asks slowly. I stay silent, but she's waiting me out.

"Cameron is okay, even though we have nothing in common. He lives in a trailer park, works a dirty job, and has a couple of kids already, even though he's just twenty-three."

"Tell me about your relationship with your brother," she says, once again taking notes.

"Cam's older than me. He was into sports and I never was, much to my dad's disappointment."

"What do you mean?" she asks, no doubt proud she got me to say the magic word—*dad*.

"I was a sickly kid. I had ear infections, asthma, allergies, and except for watching wrestling on TV, I had no interest in sports. I never played baseball or football with the guys."

"What kind of stuff did you like to do growing up?" She's really good at this.

"I liked to read, watch movies on TV, that kind of stuff. Sometimes I'd see neighbor kids outside playing ball, but it just never interested me. I spent lots of time in the house, and when my little sister, Robin, was born, I became her best friend. I babysat a lot because Mom and Dad worked all the time, whenever they could find work, but now Robin's into her own friends."

"You work a lot here at school, like in theater. Tell me about that," she says.

"When I got in sixth grade, we had a teacher who wanted us to put on a Christmas play. I figured if I did the play, then I had a reason to give my dad for not playing basketball, which he was pushing me to do. Then we did another play, and this time I got a chance to sing, and I found something else that I could do pretty well. All through junior high, I did everything I could to be onstage or perform. Then, I got the lead in a couple plays here."

"Your father must be very proud of you."

"Not really," I say, shaking my head. "He's not proud of me at all."

"I'm sensing a lot of anger at your father," Mrs. Pfeil says, acting as if she has discovered some big revelation. She may as well jot down in her notes, "Bret breathes air."

"I love him because I have to," I announce, giving words to all this hurt, saying to Mrs. Pfeil what I hold back from my father, like he holds back from me. "I respect him because he demands it, but I don't admire him, and he certainly doesn't admire or respect me."

"It seems like the two of you don't understand each other very well," she offers.

"That's what I hate the most," I confess. "He doesn't understand me. It's such a cliché. I think I hate that most of all. I want to avoid acting out any cliché. And I hate that he hates me."

"That's pretty strong, Bret, don't you think?"

"If you ask him, he'd say that he loves me, but the only reason for this is because I'm his kid. That's not love, that's obligation, and I don't want it. But personally, I know he hates me."

There's silence, because there's nothing left to say. I'm glad I got it out in the open. I don't talk about home much with Kylee because it just bores her, and I can't say that I blame her.

"Bret, I think it would be helpful if you brought your parents in to talk with me," Mrs. Pfeil finally says. "Or maybe I can recommend a good family counselor?"

"Riiiiiiiiiight," I say but she doesn't get the reference. "Who is going to pay for that?"

"If you can't talk to a counselor about this, then you can always talk to me," she says with genuine warmth, as she rises from her chair, signaling that I need to get back to class. "You can come and see me without Mr. Morgan telling you to. You know that, right?"

"I guess," I reply with a shrug. I get up to leave, feeling both weak and powerful.

"There is one other person I think you need to talk to about this," she says in closing.

"Who?"

nailed

"Your father," she replies firmly.

"He doesn't listen and you must not, either," I respond sharply, feeling almost betrayed.

"I heard everything you said and your father would too, if you would talk to him," Mrs. Pfeil says. "I know you can do it. The person you told me you admire is resilient and fearless."

"The only thing I need to learn is to fit in, get along, and go along!" I'm almost shouting now. "That's what everybody wants, isn't it?"

"No, that's not right. It's about what you want," she says. "It's your choice, but you still have to learn to obey the rules. School is like any society and you have to follow the rules."

"What I want is to get out of Flint. That's the bottom line because Bret Hendricks said so!" I throw my arms up in the Stone Cold salute once again, but this time she's not laughing.

"Bret, this isn't wrestling, this is real," she counters, trying to calm me down.

"Whatever," I say, then gather my books. Maybe today I learned the answer to my dad's question of 'Bret, what the hell is wrong with you?' What's wrong is that I'm sixteen and my father hates me. Mrs. Pfeil may know her stuff, but she doesn't know shit about my dad.

Eleven

'll see you in about thirty, okay, K?"

"Too cute, cutie," Kylee whispers, then I hang up the phone. I shoot Robin a dirty look as she and her friends giggle at me. Hell, they giggle at everything. Kylee, my source of laughter and love, is coming to take me to the opening night for my school's fall play. She's driving her mom's car, an old Honda Civic we call the snotsmobile, due to its ugly mucous green color.

Sometimes I think her voice is all that gets me through the days when we are apart. I kind of like the whole mystique of the girlfriend at the different school, but it would be great if I could see Kylee every day. I'm hungry for her, and she's starved for attention. Unfortunately, my refusal to bend to my father's will is still keeping me from getting behind the wheel, and that combined with play practice is killing our chances for one-on-one time. Ever since our first gig, she's been hanging out at Sean's place during band rehearsals, but it's not the same.

My mom can't come to the show tonight. She just started working a new night shift at Wal-Mart and can't ask for it off, but she says she will come to the matinee next weekend. I had left two tickets on the kitchen table, and as I talked with Kylee on the phone, I noticed that one remained untouched.

nailed

It's Friday and Dad's in the garage working on the Camaro. Under the hood, he listens to the engine hum; that's the music he cares about, not mine. He could listen to those pistons sing all night long, but not to me. I take the ticket in my hand; for a thin, little piece of card stock, it seems so heavy. I'll take the first step, just to let Mrs. Pfeil know she's wrong.

I walk out to the garage through a light rain. He got home from work a few minutes before I got home from school. He had his coffee, looked through the mail, cursed the bills, mumbled a few words to Mom, then headed to the garage. He'll be in for dinner at 5:30, clad in overalls, grease, and bliss, but I can't wait. We have a 5:00 stage call, and Kylee is coming over at 4:00 for some foreplay. I walk inside the garage but stay near the door of his domain. He's allowed in my room anytime for any cause, but I need a reason to enter the Camaro kingdom. I stand by the bumper, waxed so thoroughly it reflects me better than any mirror.

"Dad, here's your ticket for tonight's show." I say each word slowly and with meaning.

He grunts, so I know he hears me, yet his head remains obscured by the hood.

"Dad, I want you to come see me in the show tonight."

"Busy."

"Please."

"Busy."

I take a step closer, keeping my distance from this distant voice and the scratchless surface of his most loved object, which is so obviously not me.

"Dad, please, this is important to me."

"I said I'm busy. Maybe, if you want to help me clean this carburetor?"

His sentence fades out, transforming itself into an odd

marriage of disbelief and dismay. He knows I not only can't clean a carburetor but that I can't even identify one.

I want to grab the keys from his pocket and drag them across the pristine paint job. I want to smash the windshield glass that's so clean it's almost invisible. I want to slam the hood, and if his head's underneath . . . then all the better. I want him to stop killing me by being dead.

"I have to go. We have a five o'clock call and Kylee's on her way over to pick me up." I move two steps closer, my hand outstretched. "Here's your ticket."

He sticks his head out from under his church of worship, but never looks at me, the heathen in his Camaro cathedral. The grease transfers from his hands to a rag, but his eyes never transfer to me. The cement at his feet seems to captivate him more. He keeps his hands busy working the rag back and forth, but he never reaches to take the ticket.

I don't say anything. The engine purrs, and the rain taps against the garage windows, creating a sad vacuum of silent sound.

I say with my voice cracking, "Please." But the words don't matter. He's deaf to me or I'm dumb to him. Dumb, and becoming dumber as I continue speaking with far more emotion than is usually allowed in my father's presence. "Please, just this once."

"Are you crying?" My father asks few real questions of me. The less we talk, the less we argue. Sometimes I hate the silence more than I hate him screaming at me. Even after sixteen years, I'm still not immune to his elevated volume or his escalating indifference.

I stop speaking when he takes the greasy rag and rubs it under my eyes, taking the damp stain he finds as evidence of my disgrace. I catch a glimpse of myself in the Camaro's bumper; I look like an accident victim with two black streaks under my eyes.

"Be a man, Bret. For God sakes, be a man." He tosses the rag into the corner, as if it's contaminated with my little boy—no, my little girl—tears. "Stop crying."

"I just want—"

"Want? Who said you get what you want? Not me." He makes eye contact, but it isn't about comfort, it's about power. He digs into his overalls and fires up a Marlboro.

"Just this once," I sputter, no music in my voice, only discord. My theatrical ability to project so the back row can hear me is useless. My acting skill is now just another tool, like the ones scattered around this garage that I am too stupid to know how to use.

"You look like . . . like . . . hell," he spits out. "I don't even know what you look like!"

I've let my hair grow longer, and my ponytail now has a blue streak for Kylee to tug.

This is not a conversation, it's the script for a two-man play starring my dad and me. It's a script I have memorized. He blows out a perfect circle of smoke. The shape fits him, since my father loves going around in circles. Most summer Saturday nights, he's out with his poker pals at the Dixie Speedway watching cars spin the cement loop. On Sundays, he watched the same thing on a larger scale, courtesy of NASCAR on TV. And, of course, there's the circle of this merry-go-round we find ourselves on, as he again asks me, "What are you doing with yourself?"

I don't have an answer, and he doesn't want one. My silence shouts at him, but he doesn't raise his voice, since he's so lowered his expectations of me. "If you're going to swim upstream, don't expect it to be easy. Life is hard enough, why you want to make it harder is beyond me."

"I know," I reply meekly, showing no strength, even as I pick the hard way.

"So what, you think you're gonna be some Hollywood star who squats to piss?"

I once made the mistake of blurting out that fantasy ambition of anyone who ever stepped on a stage. I had also made the mistake of admitting that I didn't want to spend the rest of my life in Flint, Michigan. I'm not sure, in my father's eyes, which sin is worse. Both, for him, are acts of outrageous arrogance, revolution to his rule, and rejections of his life.

"I don't know."

"Jesus H. Christ, Bret, why can't you just act normal?" The head shaking starts, making his cigarette bob up and down like a conductor's baton. I'm supposed to follow.

"I don't know what that means," I say, deliberately escalating this battle. Let him hang on the cross of nonconformity, I won't make myself a casualty. He'll have to hammer those nails himself. I don't know why I'm different than what he wants; I just am. I just am.

"Normal, like your brother, and just lose all of *that,*" he says sharply. The smoke and flickering ashes from his gesture make it seem like he is performing a magic trick: trying to make me disappear. My dad is a fine actor in his own right. His reading of the word *that* brilliantly reduces everything I care about to insignificance.

"I'm sorry, but it's who I am."

"I didn't raise my boy to be a freak!" His voice is now louder than the Camaro. He snorts and then turns his back to me, extinguishing the cigarette into the ashtray.

"Don't call me that," I mumble.

He turns around quick, his expression remorseless. "I can't wait until you get out into the real world, and you don't have your weird friends or your mother to protect you." He's smiling; thoughts of my failed future amusing him. "Boy, you'll see I was right then."

"Maybe I will, maybe I won't." I find myself lost for any more words.

"Don't you have someplace to go? I need to get back to this," he says, almost shouting. His face is as red as that pack of Marlboros in his overalls. A three-pack-a-day man, his future hooked up to an oxygen tank seemed assured.

Before I can answer, he has a wrench in his hand and is back under the hood. Maybe I'm such a good actor because I really don't know the answer to my dad's question, What did I think I was doing with myself? I don't know who I am. However, as I crumple up his ticket, I know part of the answer. Looking straight ahead, I know exactly who I don't want to be.

I exit the garage and stand by the street, waiting for Kylee. Waiting for her to pick me up and take me away from this. I know there's a middle ground between Dad's harsh isolation and Mom's kind protection, but that part of the human highway is still under construction.

"Hey, cutie!" Kylee shouts. I'm so lost in my thoughts that I didn't see her pull up. She's dressed to kill in short black dress opening-night attire, but the way I feel she may as well be in mourning. She greets me with a kiss as I slowly climb into the car. "What's wrong?"

"Nothing, now that you're here." Before she reacts, I pull Kylee close to me. As we head out into the night, there are ten million ugly thoughts running through my mind about my dad, and three wonderful words unsaid to Kylee on the edge of my lips, as I soak in the sweet smell of clove cigarettes.

As we back out of the driveway, I look over behind me, into the garage. In this ongoing battle with my father, I've come to realize that I'll never be the victor, but tonight I've finally decided that I won't be a victim anymore. I know that no matter what I do, I can't please him or make him proud of me. Yet, even as the garage gets smaller in the rearview mirror, his image somehow looms larger and larger, and I realize that no matter how much I deny it, I can't stop wanting his approval.

Twelve

Dear Kylee,

Happy 18th birthday. Let me say this: <u>I live you</u>. I can't say I love you because I don't know what those words mean. In my house and history, they ring false. But most of all, those words—<u>love</u>, in particular—fall very short, even if I am much taller than you. <u>Bret lives Kylee.</u>

Your other presents are manufactured goods, but this is from me; from the heart. Let me be your Walt Whitman sampler. Let me sing and celebrate you. Or rather than Whitman, how about Browning who asked, "How do I love thee? Let me count the ways." Rather than counting from one to ten, how about I tell you from top to bottom?

I'll start with your hair: violet hair. It's not overdone: it doesn't look like somebody put a purple mop on your head, because you can see that beautiful brown hair (like your eyes, because I'm just ahead in describing your head; I guess I'm jumping below) peeking through. Now, your mouth, which I'm learning centimeter by centimeter (as you are, mine), is too beautiful for words. I love your mouth all on its own; even more when it's attached to mine.

From the tips of your tiny fingers down to your dancer's feet, everything in between is simply perfect. That time we showered together at your parent's house, I just watched one drop of water make its way from your neck and down your back, down, down. I wished I was that single drop of water, but then I realized if I were, I would never hear your sweet voice, and you would never make me laugh out loud. You told me once that I stood out, but I'm so glad I'm not standing out there alone, but instead sharing your laughter, your shower, and your heart.

Did I talk about your legs yet? Those beautiful legs that fly with the greatest of ease across the stage. You defy the laws of gravity—is it because you are an angel?

K, there you are from head to toe, and I haven't even talked about the best parts of you yet: your heart and how kind you are to me. Your mind and how smart, funny, quick, and sarcastic you are. Your soul, which lights a fire inside of me and keeps me burning through the long days and longer nights when we're apart, and how you make me feel part of something.

Alex is my best friend and I once envied him, his fearlessness, his talent, his wit, and that his dad wasn't around to hate him the way mine hates me. Sean is my next best friend, but I envied him as well. Not just his good looks and piles of green, but also his whole shy but confident self. He always seems to get what he wants. Anyway, I used to envy all my friends, but not anymore. Because from the first time I saw you, Kylee Edmonds, you were all that I wanted. So, now it's time for them to envy me. Now it's time for every bozo like Bob Hitchings to envy me. It's time for the thousands of men in Flint, the millions in Michigan, the millions and millions of men in the United States, and the couple billion the world over to envy me, because it's me and only me that gets to hold you. Happy birthday. You're the real thing, and I live you.

B

Thirteen

He wrote what?"

I can hear Principal Morgan through the glass window that separates the outer office from his inner sanctum. He looks like he's ready to explode. I can almost see him twitching as he reaches for the telephone to call my parents. I'm not afraid because Dad is safely at work, and Mom will support me; I can count on that. It also looks like I can count on being ousted from Southwestern. No doubt about it, this is strike three and I'm outta here.

"Don't even think about printing this!" Morgan shouts at Mr. Popham, the school newspaper adviser.

I'm glad that Morgan seems angrier with Popham than with me. I did nothing more than express myself, only to get slapped down one more time. After the fall play (*The Crucible*) wrapped last week, Mr. Douglas had some of us participate in forensic debates against each other. We didn't have a real team like other schools, although there was always money for sports squads, but Mr. Douglas wanted us to get experience doing research, thinking on our feet, and preparing arguments. He and Mr. Popham had agreed that since there was also no money for prizes, the winning debaters would get their speeches published in the school paper, since only the theater kids even got to hear our forensic gymnastics. Which was all well and good, until I won, and mentioned the unmentionable nine-letter word at Southwestern High School: *Columbine*. My winning speech was called "Dylan and Eric Were Victims Too."

It takes a while to get all of the concerned parties together, which gives my mom time to get to school. Once she arrives, they take us into a conference room. She looks upset; no doubt worried about the scene this will create at home because this is one situation we can't hide. We never lie to my dad, but we also never actually told him about my two other suspensions. Mom is good—maybe too good—about protecting me on stuff like this. She knows that fire doesn't need any more fuel, and this is gasoline.

"Bret, tell us why you decided to write this," Ms. Pfeil says, to start the meeting.

"It was a debate, and I thought it'd work best if I chose something controversial. This seemed like a good thing to write about," I respond. "What's wrong with that? I was just doing what a good debater is supposed to do."

"You are lucky, buster, that the board has yet to approve the zero-tolerance policy we have submitted to them, or you would be in jail right now for verbal assault," Morgan says, livid.

"Bob, just a second. That seems a little harsh," Mr. Douglas says, rushing to my defense. Morgan shoots Mr. Douglas a look that seems to say, "We'll talk about this later," but I know Mr. Douglas. He will be there for me, and I can tell Morgan wishes he wasn't.

"We're not going to publish this trash in the paper, right Mr. Popham?" Morgan says.

Popham doesn't respond right away. I don't know him that well, but he seems like a pretty cool guy, for a teacher. He looks confused, as he rubs his hand across his forehead.

"What about the First Amendment?" I say, breaking my silence and these chains I feel wrapped in like some high school Houdini. Morgan's a magician too, because he makes his lips disappear, as he rearranges his tie, no doubt wishing he could wrap it around my neck.

"He's got a point, Bob," Mr. Douglas says. "We said we would publish the winners, and Bret won outright. We shouldn't censor his opinion. To me, it just doesn't seem fair."

"This isn't about what's fair," Morgan says, continuing his love affair with the obvious. "This is about what is best for this school, which is my decision and not yours."

"Well, maybe the teacher's union or the ACLU would see it differently?" Mr. Douglas says almost rhetorically, as he pulls out a notepad and pencil.

"The question is moot," Morgan says. "What was your agreement, again?"

"That we would publish the speeches of the winning students," Mr. Popham replies.

"Right. As of this moment, Bret Hendricks is no longer a student here. I'm suspending him for this incident, and pursuant to board policy, this third suspension means he will be expelled from school," Morgan says, so full of my damnation I think he might crack wide open.

Finally, Mom speaks. "If you suspend him, we will sue you and the school board."

"What?" Morgan is stunned. I am too. Mr. Douglas, on the other hand, just smiles.

"I know I'm only a cashier at Wal-Mart, but I have enough common sense to know it's wrong to suspend a student for writing a speech, just because you don't agree with it," Mom replies. I don't know the family finances, but I know there's no way we can afford a lawyer. Even though my father is the poker player of the family, my mom is pretty good at bluffing. I hope Morgan can't see what I spy: her hands trembling under the table.

"You can't suspend Bret for something I asked him to do," Mr. Douglas says, stepping in front of the bullet. "If you want to suspend someone, try starting with me."

"I agree," Mr. Popham says, making it three against one, with Mrs. Pfeil undecided.

"All right then, there will be no suspension at this time," Morgan says after a long pause. "But what you don't understand, Mrs. Hendricks—"

"I do understand," Mom, says cutting him off. "You don't understand my son."

Morgan looks like he's possessed by some kind of hell spawn about to projectile puke. "No, I don't understand a young man who wears his hair like a girl, dresses like a homeless person, and writes a paper glorifying mass murderers."

"Wait a minute!" I cry. "Did you even hear or read the speech?"

Mr. Popham interjects, "I told Mr. Morgan what was in your speech. It concerned me too. I believe in free speech, but in times like these, we have to be very careful."

"Then you misrepresented what I said," I counter. "This isn't fair. If I did something wrong, then punish me. But I didn't do anything wrong, I just expressed an opinion."

"A very dangerous opinion," Morgan says firmly, anxious to have the final word.

"Don't you think we're all overreacting a little?" Mrs. Pfeil asks.

"Bret, what did you say?" Mom asks, bringing herself back into the conversation. Her hand and voice are still shaking, no doubt from lack of information, as she hadn't read the speech. I usually let her read my stuff because she is really good with grammar, but this speech I held close to the heart.

"That's not the point. We will not tolerate this sort of continued antisocial behavior from your son," Morgan starts. "Perhaps we should discuss a transfer to an alternative school."

"No way!" I exclaim. I don't want to leave school, especially now that Morgan wants it.

"My son is not transferring," Mom says firmly. "Honey, tell me what you said."

"I said what happened at Columbine was terrible. I didn't say it was a good thing. I didn't say that Dylan and Eric were heroes. In fact, they were two sick mofos, and what they did was very wrong. They killed a lot of people and hurt a lot of people. But I also pointed out that how they had been treated at their school was wrong too. I said they were the first victims."

"How you can feel sympathy for those sick, twisted murderers is beyond me," Morgan says.

"Not sympathy, Mr. Morgan, but empathy. Everything that happened to them happens here, every day," I say, almost spitting out the words.

"That's not true." Morgan says, his eyes focused on his desk, not me.

I turn around and push my Kylee-matching violet-tinted ponytail aside. "Look at this."

Morgan doesn't move, but my mom stares in shock at the back of my neck, which is covered with small bruises. Hitchings has given me the school's only black-and-blue neck.

"What in the world?" Mom says. I think she's going to cry, she looks so upset.

"Bob Hitchings, every day during King's English class," I say, looking down at the floor, hating that I am admitting my helplessness. "Whenever King's back is turned, he jabs or slaps me with a pencil, sometimes a pen, sometimes his hand."

"Bret, that's terrible," Mr. Douglas says. Mr. Popham seems to nod in agreement.

"It's not just me," I say, certain that me and Hitchings aren't the only harassment duo.

"Honey, why didn't you say something?" Mom asks, the look of concern on her face obviously not shared by Morgan.

"What was I going to say?" I feel like screaming. "And to whom?"

"You should have told someone!" My mother wants to hug me, but she knows that I would die from that scene. "Did you know about this, Mrs. Pfeil?"

"No, I did not. Bret, why didn't you say anything to me when we spoke?" Mrs. Pfeil asks.

"And get Hitchings in trouble?" I say, throwing my hands in the air. "Then he would just finish the job. I figured I would take a little pain and avoid a beating. What else can I do?"

"You will talk with this student?" Mom says, looking right at Morgan.

"I'll deal with Hitchings," I say bravely, yet not knowing when and where and how.

Morgan looks like he has ten thousand volts running through him. "What do you mean by that?"

"Nothing," I say, again looking down, keeping myself grounded. Lacking resources or recourse, I let my imagination run wild, envisioning Hitchings's day of reckoning, but I know better and had to let them know too. "I'm not like them, you know that, Mom?"

"Like who?" Mom asks.

"Dylan and Eric, or any of those other kids who shot up their schools," I say.

Morgan is hanging on every word, waiting for me to hang myself, no doubt.

"I know, honey," Mom says softly.

"You know why?" I ask her, but I'm directing this at Morgan. He needs to know his police state won't be breeched, that Southwestern won't be on the cover of *Time* magazine.

"Why?" she responds, letting me tell my story.

"Because you and Dad taught me right from wrong, and that if you hurt, you don't take it out on other people," I say, sitting up straight, as I stare Morgan down. "Because even though Dad owns a rifle, I don't know where he keeps it or how to use it. I don't really care that much about Hitchings and the other bullyboys. They'll get theirs, just not from me. One day, I'll be gone from here, maybe acting on Broadway or on stage at the Whiting, but Hitchings will still be in Flint, probably working at a car wash or a 7-Eleven. He'll be jerking Slurpees for a living, and one day a stack of magazines will come in, and he'll unpack them and see me on the cover of *Entertainment Weekly* or *Rolling Stone*. And you know what? You'll still be here too, Mr. Morgan. Ten years from now, telling kids to stay in line and not disrupt your little apple-cart world. So, you see, I don't want vengeance, and I don't believe violence solves anything. What I want is a reckoning, and I'm willing to wait for it to happen."

I can tell Mr. Douglas wants to smile but, great actor that he is, he won't break his character of being the responsible adult. Deep down, I can tell he's proud of me.

"Are you through?" Morgan says, hands on hips, disgust on his dour, flat face.

"And I want my speech published," I say, my confidence growing.

"We'll discuss that later," Morgan says, meaning my part in the discussion is over. I won't push the point, although I am amazed at how easily Morgan caved when people stood up to him. I wish I could have done it by myself, but Mom made a great tag-team partner. She isn't formally educated, but she was smart enough to know when Morgan was both wrong *and* outnumbered.

"So, you're not suspending him, right?" Mom says, seeking clarification and closure.

"Not this time, but remember the school board's policy. Bret's already been suspended for his inappropriate behavior toward Coach King and the incident at Homecoming. One more strike, and he's out. And I don't expect to hear the word *Columbine* come out of his mouth again, understand?" Then Morgan leans close to me. "I'm willing to wait too."

I jam my hands into my pockets to keep my middle fingers from shooting in the air and sending me slithering from school.

"Bret, we'll work this out," Mr. Douglas says, putting his hand on my shoulder. "You've got too much talent to throw it away on something like this."

I could sense what he's really saying. If Hitchings isn't worth it, neither is Morgan. I put my hat on my head as I leave the conference room, making sure that I don't stare Morgan down, because now it's about which one of us will be the first to blink.

Fourteen

You really think I should sue the school board?"

"One hundred percent!" Mr. Edmonds says. As per usual, his enthusiasm is greater than any one man should generate without a permit. "Bret, I'm sure you would win."

"I know people at the Flint office of the American Civil Liberties Union. Let me just make the call," Mrs. Edmonds says, practically jumping up from the dining room table.

"Mom, it's okay, Bret can handle it," Kylee says, stepping in.

"One call, that's all we need to make," Mrs. Edmonds says, starting to dial her practically attached-to-her-hand cell phone. "This could be a great crusade."

"Mrs. Edmonds, it's okay," I say. Kylee's parents exhausted, entertained, and intrigued me with her mom's frequent speech making and her dad's regular forays into folk singing.

"That's what's wrong with this country!" Mr. Edmonds exclaims while pouring us each a small glass of wine, but I pass. "No respect for civil liberties and basic human rights."

Kylee's parents are what my dad calls "no-good liberal do-gooders," which is just one of the many reasons, even though Kylee and I have been dating for over four months, we've never had our parents in the same room together. I did Christmas yes-terday with my parents, then came here for leftovers that are bet-ter than my family's main course.

Their house isn't a lot bigger than ours, but it's so different, and not just because everything seems covered in cat hair. Look-ing around the house, I see how it is crammed with lots of books, but no romance novels; instead, there are tomes about history, politics, and travel. Instead of a TV blaring, classical music plays. The main features of their living room are an unabridged *Oxford English Dictionary,* an *Encyclopedia Britannica,* a framed photo-graph of Martin Luther King Jr., and the movie poster of *Fahren-heit 9/11.* The room's centerpiece is a portrait of a younger Kylee—with long, chestnut-colored hair, dancing—painted by Mrs. Edmonds. The only thing my mother paints is her nails.

"Come on, let's go," Kylee says rising from the table; my eyes follow her like always.

"Where are you two off to now?" Mrs. Edmonds asks, only she isn't grilling us; she makes it sound like wherever we're go-ing, it's going to be exciting.

"Laying down tracks," I say almost grudgingly, because I re-ally just want to stay and hang with Kylee's parents. Sean's dad has bought him new recording equipment for Christmas, so we're going to break it in by cutting songs, including a new one by Alex, for a CD Sean's mom is financing. Which pretty much sums up the band. I'm the bass in the back and booming voice in front, Alex is the vision and scribe, while Sean's the beat and bank account.

"Are you one hundred percent sure you don't want me to sing a little Dylan with your band?" Mr. Edmonds says, eliciting a sigh from his only child and a kiss on the cheek from his wife. He launches into "Blowin' in the Wind": "How many roads must a man walk down—"

"No, Daddy, that won't be necessary," Kylee interrupts, her tiny hand covering her eyes as she speaks "Besides, I'm the band's beautiful muse."

"And a muse is a terrible thing to waste," I reply quickly.

"Bret, you're so quick and clever, isn't he, Kylee?" Mrs. Edmonds says.

Kylee turns her back on her mother, then shows off a five-star eye roll, sticking out her tongue for the big finish. "Whatever you say, Mom, whatever you say."

I grab my coat and pull on my multicolored long stocking cap. Kylee frowns at me, since I've once again forgotten to help her on with her coat. These little details matter to her, but what she doesn't get is that I don't have any role models. She has these supercool, loving parents who adore her and each other, in this house filled with books, eating these great gourmet meals served with wine, and all of this culture. If my house was this huge cold front and hers the center of warmth, then it's better our folks didn't meet, because for sure there would be a storm. I liked spending time there, even if it bored Kylee. Here were people who weren't "normal" by any stretch but were still living a nice life. Hope lived.

"You wanna drive, cutie?" Kylee asks, flipping me the keys to the snotsmobile.

"Okay, K," I say, this time remembering to open the door for her.

"You didn't like the wine?" Kylee says, having noticed that I barely touched my glass.

"No, I'm just not used to parents serving wine, that's all," I say as I start the car and head off to Sean's house. "We don't serve wine in my house, not since my dad started dancing the AA Twelve Step. He quit drinking the day I was born."

"That's one way for him to never forget your birthday," Kylee says, but with a dig, since I'd almost forgotten her birthday last month in the chaos of dealing with Morgan's Gestapo tactics. I had to ask Sean to loan me fifty bucks so I could even come up with my offering of Godiva chocolates, clove cigarettes, and a poster from The Wizard of Oz, upon which I'd replaced Dorothy's face with a picture I'd taken of Kylee with Sean's digital camera. Even then, if it hadn't been for my love (sans the word) letter, Kylee wouldn't have been happy, which makes me sad. Sometimes it seems like she doesn't realize that while I live her, I also have a life without her. There are times when I think Kylee wants more than I can possibly give.

"Well, he made my sixteenth quite memorable," I say, angry that Kylee's parents trust me with the snotsmobile, while my unchanged oil-change stance keeps me stuck in the driveway at home.

"Why don't you just give in," Kylee says, rolling down the window and lighting up one of her Christmas cloves. "We can't keep taking my mom's car everywhere. It ain't no big thing."

"It is to me," I say sharply, my shivering only partially because of the chill. "K, sorry, I'm not pissed at you."

"Well, I'm pissed at my father. He can be so embarrassing sometimes," Kylee says as she snuggles against me. "Wasn't his singing just awful?"

"Well, it wasn't, as he would say, 'one hundred percent' but I've heard worse," I say. "Ever hear Sean sing? It's like a form of capital punishment."

"No, I haven't," Kylee says, puffing away. "But I was just thinking something."

"What's that?"

"I was thinking maybe I could sing a few songs at your next gig," Kylee says, rubbing her hand along my leg.

"That's an idea," I say, knowing full well my voice has just betrayed me. I'm seriously in love with Kylee, and we're going through all the motions associated with those emotions. I'm head over heels, yet my head tells me this is a bad idea, and I feel like a real heel.

"Well, think about it, cutie," Kylee says, punctuating her remark by rubbing the back of her hand against my stubbly face. Sean's dad gave him thousands of dollars in electronics for Christmas so he could explore and indulge his artistic side, whereas my dad gave me a fifty-dollar grooming kit, complete with razor, to keep my whiskers, if not my hair, short.

"You tired?" I ask. Like me, Kylee is juggling a lot. She has a full load of classes, and dance lessons with occasional performances that somehow always conflict with what I'm doing. Plus her mom always wants her to help at the Food Bank.

"Exhausted," she says. "Maybe after rehearsal, we could just go back home and sleep. It's winter break, so no school tomorrow. Why don't you spend the night? I'm sure it would be okay with my folks. They'll probably even turn down the covers."

"You mean on the couch, right?"

"No, silly, in my bed." Kylee says, grabbing my hand, and running it along her black fishnets, which snag me hook, line, and sinker. "You're kind of silly in my bed, anyway."

"And that's a good thing," I say, unsure exactly what she meant. I try to cover my inexperience by making lovemaking a laugh riot at times, although in the end, I did whatever she asked to make sure she always got the last laugh, so to speak. "I need some good things."

Kylee rubs my face. "What's bothering you, cutie?"

"I just want this dark cloud to pass over. This stuff with Morgan and my speech, the stuff with my dad, putting up with cement heads like Hitchings and Coach King. I just want it all to go away, and to not have these two stupid suspensions hanging over me. I want to go to sleep for about a year and a half, then wake up to get my diploma and put all of this behind me."

"Then don't let my mom get involved," Kylee says.

"Why not?"

"Did you see her? She'll take right over," she says. "Mom's ready to take on the world. I think she cares more about its problems than she does mine."

"She loves you to death," I say, always appealing to Kylee's addiction to affirmation.

"You don't know how right you are," Kylee says as she rolls down the window and flicks the half-smoked clove onto the highway.

"But don't you think . . . ," I start to say, trailing off as Kylee yawns, closing her eyes.

"You don't live with them, Bret. Trust me," she whispers, yawns, then zones out.

I gently rub one hand over Kylee's hair, wishing that everything could feel this nice and be this easy. I would love it if we could just keep driving, smoking, listening to music, and touching each other. I've still yet to say that four letter word because it is both too frightening and too futile, but I'm happily in love with Kylee. I edge over to say "I love you" to her, even though I know Roget's rips me off without enough euphemisms or synonyms for that eight-letter three-word statement of commitment, caring, and constant craving. It's not an announcement heard much around the Hendricks household.

nailed

My parents' relationship is like what we learned in history class about trench warfare in World War I. They're locked in a slow and agonizing battle with no clear winners or losers, just lots of suffering. It's probably hard to fight with someone you barely talk to, but it could be worse. I've never seen Dad hit Mom, or even be mean to her. His sole weapon is silence and indifference; I know those soundless slings and arrows all too well.

Their life is as follows: he comes home, performs the minimal requirements of cohabitation, and then retreats into his own private world of Camaros and home repair. He goes out with friends to play poker or watch car races. She mostly works. If there was a time when she went out with him, it must seem to both of them like a lifetime ago. And yet they stay together while lots of friends' parents, like Sean's, are coming apart.

After Robin was born, everything changed for my mom. You can see it in her eyes that Robin has become her life, in the same way that my brother, Cam, is my dad's pride and joy. I'd become an orphan in my own family. My dad had hope for me once, but he's given up on all that. He's told me he loves me and puts food on the table, but he lost interest somewhere between the time when he sat up with me when I was sick and now, when he just tells me I am sick. Although he and my mom remain married, his divorce from me seems final.

I envied Sean when his parents broke up. Both of them vie for all of his attention. It's like a bidding war, and Sean is nothing if not shrewd, playing it for all it's worth. He lives with his mom, who keeps the big house, and spends a lot of time with his dad, who keeps him happy with toys for teens. Sometimes I think hanging out with Alex and me (whom they don't like), rather than Hitchings, Bison, or the rest of the water walkers, is his way of getting back at his parents for breaking up. But the past matters not, as we drive closer to Kylee's final Christmas present.

"K, time to wake up," I say gently, stirring Kylee from her catnap.

"Can't I just sleep?" She huddles up against me. "I'm so tired."

"Let me ask you something." I pull her closer, and she purrs like one of her family's cats. I just hold her for a while. "What do you think it is to be normal?"

"Why in the world would you want to be?" she says.

"I don't know. I guess that's the problem."

"I don't think normal is that great."

"But so many people choose it," I reply.

"I don't think that's it at all. I think most everyone is normal, and some of us, for whatever reason, choose to reject that and wear ruby red slippers or old black hats."

"Well, why do we choose the hard road?" I continue, hoping that Kylee won't notice we're taking a different road over to Sean's. I have a last gift for her to unwrap.

"Now, that I can't answer," Kylee says. "Maybe when I get to college next year."

"Promise me you'll do something for me after college," I say.

"Just about anything," replies Kylee, with a kiss acting as her exclamation point.

"If you run into me in ten years, and my hair is one color and cut short, and I'm jammed into a minivan with a bunch of screaming kids in the backseat, promise me something, okay?"

"Anything, cutie," she says softly.

"That you will kill me," I say sans emotion.

"Kill you?" Kylee asks, snapping fully out of her slumber.

"I'd rather be dead than live that life," I say. "I'd rather be dead than be like my father."

"Deal!" Kylee says, and kisses me again. "And being dead is okay with you?"

"I don't want to get out of the world," I whisper.

"Then what?"

"I want to get the world out of me."

"Maybe later you can put a little of your world into me," Kylee says, tugging my ponytail.

I hug her but keep my eyes on the road as we turn down a dead-end street off Fenton Road. I spot the large concrete embankment that once said "Grand Trunk Railroad." Kylee notices we're slowing down, and my heart is beating faster as we approach my revelation celebration. "Close your eyes for a second, okay, K?"

I need her to shut her eyes before I can open my heart, even if my mouth still can't say the words. On Christmas Eve, while the whole family but me was safe at church at Midnight Mass, I enlisted Alex's helping hand, and with the leftover black paint from the Rock created a Christmas present for Kylee, sans colorful paint but loaded with colossal passion.

"Bret, what's going on?" she asks, unsure of my intentions.

I flash a bright smile, then the car's bright lights onto the concrete. The Rock is fine for temporary tattoos, but not for something lasting and deep. We may be off the beaten path, but for me, it's a sign that for the first time ever, I have pulled directly onto the human highway. I may be different, but the love I feel for Kylee is normal and enormous. "Look," I tell her.

Tears fall down from her brown rounds when she reads my words painted black, boldly, and bravely and as tall as she, on cold white concrete:

BRET LIVES KYLEE

Fifteen

ean, that's not it!"

Alex isn't happy with Sean's drumming, and he's not the only one. It's been a frustrating couple of hours, as we try to record some old songs and work on Alex's newest, "Sweetheart of the Graveyard Shift." It's a great song about his new squeeze, Elizabeth, the eighteen-year-old waitress at Venus that he finally talked into going out with him. I don't think we'll make it to see Elizabeth tonight at this rate. Maybe it's because I'm exhausted from Kylee and keeping up with school, but Sean's pissing me off, and not just tonight. The last couple of weeks, his tone at school is all sharp, but tonight he's dulled his senses with a few glasses of Jack Daniels.

"Do you want me to show you again?" Alex asks Sean, his voice saturated in sarcasm.

"I got it. Sorry, guys," Sean mumbles, an unlit clove cigarette dangling from his lips.

"You're coming in too soon," Alex says, unmoved by Sean's apology.

"Just like sex between you and Elizabeth!" Sean says, hitting the cymbal for a rim-shot effect, although he's the only one laughing. The three of us are always busting each other, but our girlfriends are usually off-limit topics. For Sean that's true, for Mr. Jack Daniels, not.

"Sean, why don't—" Alex starts.

"Guys, this isn't getting us anyplace," I say, trying to be the perfect peacemaker. "Why don't we stop trying to record new material. Let's just play an old song, to get in the groove."

"How about 'Matter of Fact'?" Alex says, tuning his guitar.

"Are you sure you trust me with your precious originals?" Sean asks, egging Alex on.

"Sean, maybe you better check where you're sitting, because I think you got a drumstick stuck up your ass!" Alex replies to Sean's whiskey-inspired insult in a voice louder and sharper than the chords he's playing. "What exactly is your major malfunction?"

"Whatever, Wordboy," Sean shoots back.

"Guys, come on," I shout. "Let's do 'Burton Calling' then. Everybody okay with that?"

"Okay, but I have a suggestion," Sean says, as he taps away on the snare.

I shoot Alex a look. I know he wants to say something but instead he just frowns and starts tuning his guitar.

"What's that?" I ask.

"Why don't we let Kylee sing background, or maybe even lead vocal?" Sean says, pointing his drumsticks at Kylee. She is blowing white clove smoke, scratching down thoughts in black ink in her purple journal, acting like the angry scene spilling in front of her isn't real.

"We don't do duets," Alex says contemptuously. "Bret, what do you think?"

I pause for a second, then ten, and then almost a minute. My mouth's closed, but it can't stay that way. I know Alex wants only me to do vocals, but I also know Kylee really wants to do this. I don't know why Sean even cares.

"Don't you wanna share the stage with us Kylee?" Sean asks in a strange tone.

"It's not that. It's just, you know, it might be kind of weird to have the two of us singing together," I say, trying to signal Kylee with my nonverbal shoulder shrug apology.

"You guys must do all your singing between the sheets," Sean says, hitting the cymbal again, then adding a drum roll. "Singing in the sheets, singing in the sheets!"

Sean laughs and so does Kylee, who puts down her journal. "What do you think?" Kylee whispers in my ear as she walks by toward the microphone.

Alex lets out a huge sigh that suggests he regrets not just getting Sean in the band, but even knowing him. I look at Alex, then smile sadly at Kylee, and finally glare at Sean.

"Forget it, wannabe," Sean says. "You don't have to sing it with her. I will."

"Now Sean, you're the funny man," I say with a sarcastic smile, winking at Alex.

"I'm serious," Sean says with an evil grin. "Kylee, you'll sing with me, won't you?"

I turn on my heel and face Sean. "Don't take this the wrong way, but just because you were born with a silver spoon in your mouth doesn't mean you have a golden throat."

"What the hell do you mean by that?" Sean says. "Can't you just say something without busting your ass to sound so damn clever?"

"Well, I'll keep it simple then. When it comes to singing, two words best describe you," I snap back. "You suck."

"And I got two words for you, wannabe: fuck you!" Sean says, flicking his cigarette my way as Kylee returns to her seat, out of harm's way.

"What is your problem!" I shout back.

"Here's two more words for you: get out!" Sean shouts, hurling both of his drumsticks my way. One misses me, while the other catches me in the gut, just above the belt. It doesn't hurt, but the pain of this is killing me. The band, our music, these guys: this is supposed to be a release from the other crap in my life, but suddenly it stinks just as bad as everything else does.

"Sean, what is your problem?" I ask, wondering where all this anger came from.

"What are you going to do, Bret, fight me or run away like you do with Hitchings?" Sean says. He laughs like it's all a joke. Guess when life is so easy, nothing ever comes down hard.

"Damn it, Sean, cool it!" Alex finally interjects.

"Big surprise, you're taking his side," Sean yells at Alex.

"What does that mean?" Alex replies, at equal volume.

"You're the musical genius, figure it out," Sean says. "Look at the two of you: Wordboy and Wannabe."

Sean stands up, or tries to anyway. He slips for a second and then rights himself, putting his fists out in front of him. "Right now, Bret, let's you and me settle this."

"I'm not going to fight you," I say, the exhaustion obvious in my face.

"Why not?" Sean shouts.

I pause, take a deep breath, and then look quickly at Alex. Before I can answer, I hear a noise. It's Kylee. I hear the smack of her journal falling on the floor, then the heel of her shoes clicking as she runs out of the room. She's fleeing the scene of my lack-of-spine crime.

"Hey, it's not like with Hitchings. I'm no jock so this will be a fair fight," Sean shouts.

Sean's shorter than me, but thicker and way tougher. "I won't fight you just because."

"Because why?" Sean challenges, unwilling to let it go or drop his fists or tough guy act.

"Because that's the bottom line and Bret Hendricks said so!" I say, doing my best Stone Cold Austin impersonation, which nobody in the band ever appreciates.

"You and your wrestling crap," Sean says. "What a welfare white trash soap opera."

The fact that his parents make in an hour what my dad does in a day has never come between us, but it's always there and comments like that don't make it easy to forget, but I let it pass. "I won't fight you. You're acting like an asshole, but you're still my friend."

"I was Alex's bud long before you. I'm his best friend," Sean responds, making it sound like a grade school playground tussle. "I'm his best friend, and you're just his freak boy-toy!"

"Freak boy?" I repeat these magic words. I held back with my dad, with Hitchings and Principal Morgan, but they aren't close to me, so their comments don't seem real. More angry than afraid, I dive at Sean. I don't want revenge, I just want a break from this rain of ridicule. Since I won't or can't fight Hitchings, I'll settle for his neighbor. Sean swings wildly, but I land a hard punch to his nose, which explodes in blood. Alex quickly jumps in and holds me back before any more punches are thrown, but I first manage to push Sean hard into his drum set and onto the floor. We're sprawled on the floor, breathing heavily, when Sean starts laughing even as blood trickles over his lips.

"Lucky punch," Sean says, then laughs. He knows he could kick my ass; so do I. Lucky punches, like lightning, strike just once.

There's quiet while Alex puts his Gibson back in the case. Sean and I sit on the floor, about ten feet apart. After a few moments, Alex taps me on the shoulder, "Come on, let's go."

I stare over at Sean. I want to be angry at him, but I'm more surprised than seething mad.

"Alex, have you seen Kylee?" I ask, my eyes still staring at Sean, who has this goofy grin on his face, like nothing happened other than maybe my lucky shot sobered him up some.

"I'll check," Alex says as he walks over to the basement window with its clear view of the driveway. While he's on the other side of the room, I decide it's gut-check time.

I get off the floor, go over toward Sean, and stick out my hand at him. "I'm sorry Sean."

He shakes my hand, double pumps it. "I'm sorry too, but one good thing came from this."

"What's that?" I ask.

But before he can answer, Alex yells, "Kylee's car is gone."

"Are you sure?"

"The snotsmobile is snots to be found," Alex says, walking back over and grabbing the Gibson. "I got you, but are you up for a visit with my sweetheart of the graveyard shift?"

"Do I have a choice?" I respond.

"No," Alex says, and we all laugh. So the evening ends on a high note, which is all I'd be singing anymore if Sean had bigger drumsticks and better aim.

"Let's call Kylee from Venus and ask her to join us, okay?" I ask Alex.

He moves his head, nodding yes, even though I know he'd rather say no. Loyal to the end friend.

"Sean you wanna come?" I ask Sean, who has relocated to where Kylee was sitting, even finishing up the rest of her smoke. He shakes his head no, then I shake his hand again, adding a high five for good measure. As Alex and I start up the stairs, I realize I've forgotten something. "Hey, Sean, you said something good came of all this?"

He laughs, then points to the trickle of blood coming from his nose. "I know how you can finally get back at Bob Hitchings."

"How?" I'm confused and Alex looks equally perplexed.

"Let him beat the shit out of you and then sue his dad's rich ass," Sean says with a laugh.

"One problem with that plan," I note. "There's a name for me getting into a fight with Bob Hitchings."

"And what's that?" Alex butts in.

I pause just for a second before I speak. "Suicide."

Sixteen

What's the problem now, Hendricks?"

My behavior was severe enough for King's eyes to make a rare appearance from behind his newspaper. Another day of English class goes by with us silently reading from the required novel, *The Grapes of Wrath,* while Mold King Cold does his required *USA Today* sports score reading and crossword puzzle. A new year begins the same as the old one ended.

"None, sir," Hitchings replies, reclining back in his chair and stuffing the lighter he'd been flicking in my ear back into his pants.

"I want to change my seat," I say, grabbing my books and jumping from my chair.

"Seats in this room are assigned by me," Mr. King announces. "Sit back down, Hendricks!"

"No, I'm not sitting here anymore," I say in a calm and nondefiant tone.

"Do you want to go take another trip to see Mr. Morgan?" Mr. King asks.

"No, I want Hitchings to stop trying to light my hair on fire," I say, turning around and pointing at him. Despite the new tangerine streak in my hair, I don't want it to become burnt orange tinged and singed.

Mr. King makes the ultimate effort of tearing himself away from his newspaper and walking over to us. "And how is he doing that? By rubbing two sticks together?"

"No, only Sean the drummer boy can do that," I say, shooting Sean a smile, in hope that Sean will come to my defense, but he avoids eye contact. Even though we made up after the fight, there's still some tension with Sean, and with Kylee. She told me that the angry side of me she saw at rehearsal that night scared her. We made up with a make-out session in the snotsmobile the next day, but since then, it seems likes she's been avoiding me.

"I'm not doing anything," Hitchings says, the glow of innocence lacking from his face.

"He's got a lighter in his pocket," I say, pointing to Hitchings's perfectly pressed prep pants.

"Stop looking at my crotch," Hitching says loudly enough for everyone to hear. It gets a laugh. He silently mouths "faggot" for my fringe benefit only.

"Bob, I'd need a microscope to see something that small," I reply, and it gets a colossal cackle from the class. Lots of the non-water-walker students in class are laughing the loudest.

"That's enough, the both of you," King says. I'm not sure who got to him, or maybe it's just what passes for his conscience, but he's let up on me since that rough beginning of the year. Maybe because I hadn't bothered to fight or talk back again. I just took it, until today.

"Just search him, you'll find the lighter," I say, still keeping a safe distance in case Hitchings decides to take a swing at me with one of the meaty paws now hidden in his pockets.

King's smile is crooked. "Well, Mr. Hendricks, that would violate his civil rights. From what I hear from Mr. Morgan, you know all about these constitutional issues."

Hitchings guffaws. I sigh, surrender, and then sit back down, closing up *The Grapes of Wrath*. I'm like the book's protagonist, Tom Joad, with Hitchings as my personal dustbowl.

I don't bother to go back to reading, since I read Steinbeck's masterpiece last summer. I put my head down on the desk and imagine I'm resting in Kylee's arms. I don't fall asleep, but daydream of a better place. Like the Joads, I'm looking for a promised land far away from Flint.

When the bell rings, I make a quick exit, then wait for Sean outside the door.

"Sean, what gives?" I ask. "I thought we were cool."

"It's all good," Sean replies, cool and clichéd. "Look, I gotta get to my next class."

"Thanks for backing me up in there, NOT!" I reply, not getting the hint.

"What can I say?" Sean says. "I don't want to get involved. You know that Hitchings lives around the corner from me. His dad and mine are pals. I just want to stay out of it."

"What if he'd torched my hair?" I ask.

"You didn't need me. You nailed him," Sean says with a cheese-eating grin.

"What?" I reply.

"You're right about Hitchings, you know," Sean says, leaning in closer, the smell of clove cigarettes still lingering from his before-school smoke. "I had gym class with him last year. He's got a little bitty worm down there, not like the monster between your legs."

My face turns red as Sean gives me a good-natured slap on the back. "Thanks, I think."

"What are friends for?" Sean says.

"Oh, one more thing: I thought of a little problem with your master plan."

"My what?"

"Remember? Getting Hitchings to fight me for the lawsuit," I say. "Even if I wasn't at fault, I'd get suspended for fighting. It'd be my third strike, and I'd be out of school."

"Well, that's one way to get out of homework," Sean says as the bell rings. "It took some real stones to stand up to Hitchings and King like that. Sorry I didn't have your back."

"There's always a next time, so you owe me," I reply, and he winks in return. I've got to do something to avoid there being a next time, since Hitchings isn't going away. So, rather than heading toward second period theater class with Mr. Douglas, I walk toward Mrs. Pfeil's office.

"Come on in, Bret," Mrs. Pfeil says, surprised to see me. This is the first time I've ever seen her other than as a result of Morgan's prime directive. "What can I help you with today?"

"I have to get out of Mr. King's English class," I say, quickly sitting down, and settling down with a deep breath. "Transfer me when the new semester starts later this month."

"You know that's hard to do," Mrs. Pfeil says, punching something into her keyboard. "You need to learn to get along with your teachers, even if you don't like them or think they play favorites."

"Okay, fine, in that case, I want to drop the course, take an F, and repeat it over the summer because if not, I'm going say something raw to King," I say, clumsily improvising a solution.

"Which would lead to your third suspension," she adds, although we both know the truth and consequences. "Contrary to what you believe, nobody, even Mr. Morgan, wants that."

"I don't believe you," I say under my breath.

"Bret, you're very bright, talented, energetic, and creative, but—"

"Keep going, keep going," I say, encouraging her with my hands.

"But you're only one student," Mrs. Pfeil continues. "Mr. Morgan has to worry about the fate of eight hundred students here at Southwestern, so I hardly think he has the time to single you out."

"You ever heard of Delmore Schwartz?" I ask, not giving her time to answer. "He's this great American poet who wrote a book called *In Dreams Begin Responsibilities,* and he said 'Even paranoid people have real enemies.'"

She laughs. "Point well taken. Not true in this case, but well taken."

"Mr. King doesn't like me," I remind her. "I want to make sure that nothing happens, so I don't lose control and get expelled."

"Maybe this is a valuable lesson in self-control," she says. I want to tell her: Look, lady, I've lived with someone who hasn't had a drink in sixteen years, so I know all about self-control.

"Then get me out of his class because I'm not learning anything. Look, a new term is starting and I want a fresh start. Isn't there anything you can do?" I'm barely disguising my desperation.

"You feel like starting the new year with some new goals?"

"Yes, Mrs. Pfeil," I don't mean to sound sarcastic; I just do. But she's right, it's insane to do the same things and expect different results. I'm giving myself a constant headache running headfirst into the brick walls: I can't fight, I'm tired of freezing, so all that's left is to flee.

"Okay, I'll see what I can do." She takes a pass out of her desk drawer for me to hand off to Mr. Douglas. For every King, there is a Pfeil or a Douglas.

"Look, I'll be happy just to get to a state college, but I need another English teacher other than Coach King," I say, even knowing that I would need an academic scholarship in order to go to college to study theater. Dad has told me he won't put a cent toward me studying "that acting crap" and I know most schools would much rather hand out scholarships to helmet heads like Hitchings rather than stage stars like me. Dad's only offered to help foot the bill if I learn a trade.

"Like I said, let me see what I can do," she says, and I believe her, even if Stone Cold Steve Austin's motto of DTA (Don't Trust Anyone) is a good one.

"I'll take any class first period if you can get me out of there."

"Anything?" she repeats mischievously.

"Okay, maybe not woodshop," I say and then laugh, eliciting a smile from her.

"You sure that wouldn't appeal to you, Bret?"

"I think I already know everything I'll need to know about that."

"Oh?" She opens a file drawer, and I hope it's to grab a class-change form.

"My dad taught me that if you can't do something right, do it wrong with a hammer."

She nods and laughs. "My father taught me the same thing."

"He's also teaching me that the nail that sticks out the farthest gets hammered hardest."

"I've never heard that one," she comments as I get up to leave.

"He teaches me that every day, in one way or another."

"You see, maybe your dad has a lot to teach you," she says as I leave her office.

"I guess," I mumble. My head hurts not just from my dad's hammering and yammering, but from the hard truth that lies in that cliché. He's not going to change and neither is the world, so I have to. He hasn't been talking about the oil in the car, but the same stubborn blood running through both his veins and mine.

Seventeen
February 12, Early Evening, Junior Year

ret—you sure you want to do this?"

"One hundred percent!" I shout as I put the third and final box of books and videos into the back of Alex's car. "Let's get moving."

"Moving you away from Monday night TV!" Alex says as we speed off from my house to Jellybean and toward a break with my past. I'm selling my wrestling videos (except Summer Slam 1997) and my books (except Steinbeck) to get money to buy Kylee the perfect Valentine's Day present. But it's not just about money, it's also about budgeting my time. With the winter musical coming up, the band needing more rehearsals, more shows for me to usher at Whiting, and Kylee wanting and deserving more attention—not to mention school—I need more time in my life. So I'm laying the smackdown on watching wrestling. We're also doing this on Monday, since I want to make sure I don't run into Kylee because some of the stuff I'm selling are gifts from her to buy her something nice in return. I'm safe because she's helping her mom at the Food Bank, as she's done every Monday night since Christmas.

"Hey, listen to this new demo," Alex says, pulling a tape from his bowling shirt pocket.

"Another ode to Elizabeth?" I ask, already knowing the answer.

"There is no other," Alex says, popping in the tape and turning up the volume. I pull the fedora over my eyes so I can concentrate on the music. I dare not speak. Alex believes his demos, like his songs, are sacred texts deserving praise, attention, and then more praise. I try to focus. It's obvious he's written another hook-filled gem. I'm bopping my head as I scratch the stubble on my face, which I intend to keep. After Jellybean, I'm going to return the razor my dad gave me for Christmas, and take the fifty bucks over to Sean's to pay him back for Kylee's birthday-gift loan. Even though it's February, I feel like I'm starting the New Year fresh and focused.

Mrs. Pfeil is helping me with that, since she kept her word and got me transferred into Mr. Popham's English class. The pluses are I know people in there. There's Becca Levy and her buddy Will Kennedy. He's always seemed like just another jocko yahoo, but maybe I've been judging him by his clique instead of his capabilities. The minus is that the class is second period, which means I needed to drop Mr. Douglas's theater class. I hated bringing him the news, but he was cool about it, reminding me that he's casting the after-school winter musical *Bye Bye Birdie* next week, and there's a great role for me as the Elvis character. He tells me the audition is a formality. He also wants me to get Alex to play in the orchestra. The thought of Alex in a tux playing show tunes on his Gibson is pretty funny.

"What do you think?" Alex says as the song finishes. I know there's only one answer.

"Genius," I say, and it's true, even if my brain didn't lie still while I listened.

"You think?"

"I know," I reassure him. "Better than ninety-nine percent of the crap on the radio."

"That doesn't take much," Alex says, setting himself up to launch into another lengthy and lively rant about the miserable state of modern music. "Nothing is original and—"

"Let me ask you something," I interrupt his monologue, because he made me think about my dialogue with Kylee a while back. "Alex, what do you think it's like to be normal?"

"It's like a sweater: it fits, it's comfortable, and it's boring," he says, matter-of-factly.

"Really?"

"I don't plan to get married, have 2.3 children, live in the suburbs like Sean, vacation in Cancun, that whole SUV-powered super-success plan." Alex launches an all-new tirade, but his offensive outpourings seem to be a great defense against people who make fun of him.

"And why's that?"

"I couldn't afford it for one thing, and for another, I don't have the wardrobe. I mean, look at me!" Alex, who isn't ashamed of who he is, like I am sometimes, is quite the sight today. Ratty jeans, a Goodwill-issue well-worn black T-shirt with red writing that says "Spear Britney," and new antique granny glasses. Unlike me, he has so many piercings, it's a wonder he doesn't rust when it rains. His growing beard hides his pockmarked face perfectly. "Why do you ask?"

"I just wonder what it'd be like to be one of the normal kids at school," I say, thinking about Sean, who blends into the school scene, even if he merges into our musical mix.

"Why are you so hung up on being normal?" Alex asks the question that haunts me.

"Take Sean, for example," I reply, green envy coloring my words. "He knows people find him attractive, and he's sure that his shy-guy routine will always get him the girl."

"But I already got the girl, and so do you," Alex says, and shrugs.

"Maybe it's like Dad says: there are two ways to do things— the easy way and the hard way. I guess normal would be the easy way," I finish.

"Look, I don't know why I'm one way and everyone else is another, it just is," Alex says. "But I know this: high school is only four years of my life. Hell, people have survived war, famine, and a lot worse than Bob Hitchings for a lot longer than four years, and he—"

"Ain't shit," I say as Alex pulls into the Jellybean parking lot and I prepare to shed some of my self in return for cold hard cash.

I do great at Jellybean, where the clutter and smell of used books well-read overwhelm and excite the senses. I'm able to part with everything, except for clutching on at the last second to my beat-up copy of *Fight Club* with the sex scenes underlined. I resist the lure of several CD purchases by Ann Arbor indie bands for sale at the counter, and pocket my profit.

We next stop at the Wal-Mart where my mom doesn't work to return the razor.

Later, counting the green, it looks like I've got fifty bucks for Sean, and another fifty for Kylee's Valentine's gift. I need also to right the wrong of not wanting her to sing with the band, so I'm two in the hole. Maybe I'll take Alex's idea and pen a song about her. Now that Sean and I are good again, he might let me use his equipment to record it. I'll ask him tonight. Yes, this is shaping up to be a perfect Valentine's Day. Sometimes, I guess, normal is nice enough.

"Let's head over to Sean's, then we'll go to Venus to see Elizabeth," I say, and Alex nods in agreement. A light snow is falling, so he's driving slowly. I like riding with Alex more than Sean, who always plays his music so loud while he drums on the dash with a stray hairbrush. Like us, he must dream of busting out of Flint, becoming a star, and touching the sky.

Then I see it in Sean's driveway: Kylee's snotsmobile. And in an instant, I know.

"Stop the car," I shout, not even waiting until he does to jump out. I look in Kylee's car, but it's empty. The house looks empty too, but I see lights in the basement. I run over to the basement windows and kneel down in the fresh wet snow. I look in to see that I'm not the only one on my knees. I can't see much of Kylee from here, but probably more than Sean can view of her. Right now, all Sean can see is the violet hair on the top of Kylee's head and her tiny hand stroking him as the sky falls on me.

"Bret, what's wrong?"

Before I can answer Alex, I turn away from the basement window, stagger a few feet back toward the driveway, and leave my macaroni-and-cheese dinner in a steaming yellow bile pile in the gathering snow. I wipe my mouth off, catch my breath, and wish I were dead.

"What's Kylee's car doing here?" Alex innocently asks; he hasn't seen what I've seen. It's an image I'll never forget as long as I live, which, with any luck, won't be much longer.

"Are you okay?" Alex asks as he walks over toward me. I motion for him first to be silent, and then wave at him to stay away. He catches on that something is very wrong and gets back in the car. I sit in the snow, rocking back and forth, holding my arms tight around my wet knees, trying to fight off the panic that washes over me like the falling February snow.

"Let's go," Alex says as he taps me on the shoulder. I didn't hear him get back out of the car, but now he's beside me. He sticks out his hand and helps me up, then we walk back to his wheels. He slides in front, while I crawl in the back and collapse into a fetal ball.

"What the hell's going on?" Alex asks forcefully.

"Just drive!" I shout, my throat sore from swallowing tears and tossing my dinner. My lungs are burning, my hands are a block of ice, and my heart is broken. Kill me now.

"Where to?" Alex asks in a quiet, respectful tone.

"I don't know yet," I reply, trying to think if there's a steep enough cliff in all of Flint.

"Bret, talk to me," Alex says, but he's not pushing.

"Kylee and Sean," I say. The image of Kylee with Sean churns like acid in my stomach.

"What do you mean?" Alex says. Is he that clueless or that trusting? Or maybe he already knows. He's got more history with Sean, so why wouldn't he turn on me like Kylee?

I bite down hard on my bottom lip until I can taste blood. I don't want to scream at Alex. I just want to die in order to escape from this nightmare.

"I'm taking you home," Alex says. "I don't know what else to do with you."

"Kylee and Sean," I repeat, stunned by the words and the dislocation of Sean's name paired next to Kylee's. "She was . . . she's cheating on me. He's cheating on me."

"God, Bret, I'm sorry," Alex says, pulling the car off the road. "I didn't know."

"Swear on your father's grave." I reach out and grasp the handle of the car door, because if Alex knew about this, I will exit the çar and become a speed bump on the highway. The pain of getting run over would be better than facing that kind of betrayal.

Alex turns to face me, and then reaches out to touch my shoulder. "Bret, I swear."

"Thank you," is all I can say because I can't fall any farther into this abyss.

"I can't believe it. That rich spoiled prick!" Alex says, slamming his fist on the dash.

I sit up in the seat. Headlights from an oncoming car hit me right in the face and clear what is left of my mind. The fight Sean and I had the day after Christmas . . . some other remarks . . . obviously I was so blindly in love with Kylee that I was also deaf and dumb. Now, once again I'm mute. I lie back down, and Alex takes that as his cue to get restarted on the journey home. I close my eyes tightly, which holds back tears, but not the image of Kylee and Sean.

"We're here," Alex announces minutes later, his voice echoing my exhaustion. He gets up and opens the door, then helps me out. "Anything you need, you call."

I give him a big hug, and then lose it. I cling to Alex like I'm drowning and he's a life jacket. After a while, I let him go. He gets back into his car and drives home, leaving me standing alone in the stone-cold darkness of the night. I look inside the house and see no lights on. Although Mom's home from work, she and Robin have already gone to bed. I pull the key from my coat and take a step toward the door but stop in my tracks when I see a light still on in the garage. I'm drawn moth-to-flame toward it, my father, and simple, raw catharsis.

I don't even knock as I barge into my dad's sanctuary. He's sitting on a stool next to his workbench, smoking a cigarette, flipping through a car magazine, and sipping from a white coffee cup.

"What are you doing in here?" he asks, closing the magazine and straightening up.

I don't say anything. I stomp the length of the garage and flip on the large overhead light, then open the door to my mom's car. I pop the hood open and go to the front, jamming my fingers under the hood as I look for the release latch.

"I asked you a question," my dad says.

"I'm changing the oil like you wanted!" I shout at him. "Where's the fucking filter!"

"What'd you say?" he replies, more surprised than angry.

"Just give me the oil filter," I repeat, my volume on overdrive. "You want me to change the oil, fine. I'll change the filter. Why? I know. Just because!"

"Help yourself," he says as he unlocks a cabinet and tosses the filter my way. I catch it, then throw my coat and hat onto the filthy floor, while he gathers the oil and a funnel. I need to remember what to do; I need to block out the image of Kylee and Sean. Kylee and Sean.

"Hey, be careful—" my dad says, but I don't give him a chance to finish.

"I'll do it myself, isn't that what you want?" I tell more than ask. "All by myself."

"Don't mess it up," he says, like he expects I will. I crawl under the car. I'm under for just a few seconds, when he taps my foot, then hands me a flashlight. "This'll make it easier."

It takes me about an hour, forty-five minutes more than Cameron's shop guarantees, but I manage to complete the task without help. When I finish, I hand him the flashlight. I'm covered in sticky, smelly black oil and still unreleased red-hot anger. "Happy now?" I spit out, dramatically putting out my left hand, palm facing upward.

"As a matter of fact, yes," he says, his weathered face creasing into a melancholy smile. It is a smile that says "I won" yet seems to acknowledge that I look as ludicrous as his ridiculous requirement. I'm filthy, but we both seem to know that I've come clean and he's broken me.

"The keys," I say, pushing my hand closer.

My dad looks me over and then reaches into his pocket. He pulls out his big NASCAR keychain chock-full of metal, because everything in the garage has a lock. He starts to fiddle with it, placing two keys in my hand. I casually snatch a cigarette from his pack.

"Here," he lights up the smoke for me, then does the same for himself. "It's too late and too snowy for you to drive tonight."

"Fine," I say, pulling the smoke into my lungs in a slow-motion suicide.

"Ask your mom about her work schedule, maybe you can drive to school tomorrow," he says, forcing out something resembling a smile. "That is, if the roads are good. You don't know how to drive in the snow. Nobody in Michigan knows how to drive in the snow, anymore."

"Fine," I say, although I know I can't go to school tomorrow and face seeing Sean.

"How many?" he says, tapping his Marlboros.

"Maybe two packs a week," I reply, waiting for my punishment or a pissed-off look.

"It'll kill you, you know," he says. I think about being dead, and I take another puff, which floats around in the silence.

"So?" my dad finally shatters the stillness.

I shake my head. To speak of it will cause tears, and to cry would undo everything.

"Bret, what the hell's wrong with you tonight?" he's almost shouting, but not in anger.

"Like you really care," I say bitterly, showing off the key to Mom's car. "I changed the oil, and we both got what we wanted. You can stop pretending like my life matters to you."

He just glares at me, no doubt trying to pick the right cruel remark from the many dancing through his head, so I turn to leave. I get about six steps away.

"I'm your father, Bret, of course I care," he says, his tone no longer brisk, his anger having changed like the oil into something approaching sympathy.

"I don't want to talk about it," I say, my eyes facing away from him.

"I know you don't," he says, and I turn now to face him.

"Really?" I reply. "How's that?"

"I was sixteen too," he says, almost a whisper, like he's telling me a shameful secret.

I don't know how to respond other than the regular way. "I don't want to talk about it."

"And that'll kill you quicker than these," he says, taking a deep drag on his cigarette, then holding it up in front of my face.

"Good," I say, as the thought of suicide brings relief, not fright.

"Jesus H. Christ, talk to me, Bret," he says, taking a swig from the coffee cup.

"I don't know where to begin," I confess, waiting a few minutes before sitting down on the stool next to him. I'm about the same height as my dad, but tonight he seems much taller. I've lost everything that matters, so I may as well try for something that

I've never had. If ever I needed my father to be there, it's here and it's now.

My dad gives me time and space as he walks to the other side of the garage to turn off the overhead light. He pops the hood again, and looks inside. He smiles. "Good job, son."

"It's my girlfriend, Kylee," I say, measuring each word so they were close enough to keep the tears from spilling out. Letting them take over would be the easy way. This is something worth doing the hard way.

"And?" Dad's only met Kylee a few times. He took one look at her violet hair, and she didn't stand a chance. He's been civil, but not accepting and loving like her parents are with me. But then I've never seen my dad be that way with anyone, except his poker pals.

I try to speak, but I can't. My father sits back down, but even though he's trying to be considerate, I can't escape the feeling that this person across from me is a stranger.

"She pregnant?" he asks, his voice sounding strangely tired.

"No, she's not," I say, trying to keep my balance. "I mean—"

"You're having sex, right? Don't lie to me, Bret."

"Yes, but we use, you know, protection." I say, feeling unprotected as I say the words.

"I know, your mother found a condom wrapper in the laundry a couple of weeks ago," he says, with a laugh. "I said I would talk to you, but—"

"We don't really talk, do we?" I say, accepting my responsibility. My folks never had the big sex talk with me. Not that it would have mattered. I would have done everything the same with Kylee, except now I wish that I had never met her. "You're not pissed?"

"Your mother is, but I'm not," he says. "You know why?"

I can only shake my head and tap out some more ash.

"Because you're not being stupid about it." He takes another drink. "Unlike me."

"I don't understand," I say, words falling far short of describing this unreal scene.

"You know that I got your mom pregnant when we were just seventeen. I went to work to support my family and I haven't stopped for a day since. But you know all of that."

"Dad, I don't really know anything about you," I say with blunt force, since my brain is fried from the memory of Kylee and Sean burning hot. Then, just like Mrs. Pfeil did with me, I go silent and wait him out. We've waited sixteen years, what's a few minutes more.

"When I was seventeen, my dad and your grandfather, God rot his soul, gave me a hundred-dollar bill the day Cameron was born, telling me that was the last money I was getting from him. When I first told him your mom was pregnant, he jumped in his car and drove away," he says softly.

My father let out a loud sigh before lighting up another smoke. I passed when he pointed the pack my way. I want to concentrate as my dad dredges up the details. "He comes back an hour later, and pulls me out of the house—and I mean pulls me—I was probably bigger than him, but he was my dad. Anyway, he opens the trunk and throws out a brand-new suitcase, tells me to pack my shit, and move in with your mother, although that's not what he called her."

I don't ask, he doesn't tell.

"He's drunk and standing there in the driveway, screaming at me about what a loser I am and how I'll never amount to anything," Dad says, then looks like he wants to cry, although I don't think he actually knows how. Instead, he takes a drink to add fluids. "And he was right."

I'm feeling short of breath. My heart is pumping so hard it's compressing my lungs.

"Your grandpa died when you were two, so you never knew him. You didn't miss anything. He was a loser too." Dad says. "He wasn't religious, like your mom. He'd never set foot in a church except to get married, and then thirty years later, to get buried. When he died, the priest asked me to help with the eulogy. He asked what kind of man my dad was."

My dad could have been an actor. I didn't realize he's such a good storyteller.

"And I remember, like it was yesterday, although it's been over fourteen years now, what I said when the priest asked me what kind of man your grandfather—what kind of man my father was." He takes a drag to steady his voice, and another drink from his coffee cup to clear his throat. "I said this: 'He's one mean, rotten, drunk son of a bitch, and I'm glad he's dead.'"

For the second time this evening, I'm too shocked to speak.

"Maybe I should have told you this before. I know you think I'm a son of a bitch, and you know what? You're right. I am. In fact, that's all I know." He scratches his forehead, but I think he's really hiding the emotion in his eyes. "So what's wrong with you and Kylee?"

"She's cheating on me with my friend Sean," I say, the weight still heavy but somehow less crushing. I can almost breathe again.

"I'm sorry, son," he says and puts his hand near the middle of the workbench. He can't bring himself to touch me, but he wants to connect. It's enough.

"It's not fair," I say, the dam bursting. He just lets me cry out without comment.

"Bret, I want you to remember something," he says, when he thinks I can hear again. "I had to go to work at seventeen, and I've never had anything. My dad was a drunken piece of shit, and I swore I'd do better. I had a few good years, just a taste of a good life—I was able to buy my Camaro, just like the one I always wanted when I was your age—when that taste of an easy life got slapped right out of my mouth. They shut the plant down, and I was out of work with kids, a wife, a mortgage, and a drinking problem," Dad says, trying to find a comforting voice after so many years of using a caustic one toward me. "You learned how to change the oil on the car, and that's a good lesson. Well, here's another one: life isn't fair. That's a hand you can always bet on."

I look at my watch. It's almost two in the morning on the longest day of my life. The worst day of my life; the best day of my life.

My dad picks up his cigarettes and magazine, and motions for me to come to the door. I get up, but in my sleep-deprived daze and daily clumsiness, I knock over the white cup, the liquid within spills on the table, then drips down to the floor. My dad turns to look at me as I put a finger into the forming puddle of fluid, then put it to my mouth. It tastes terrible, but I've never liked the taste of coffee, even if it takes my dad Twelve Steps every day to drink coffee instead of something else.

Dad's eyes shoot right through me, and he laughs, for once not at me, but also not with me. I figure he laughs at himself and at the world. "Life isn't fair, Bret, but that doesn't mean you accept it. I'm sorry you got hurt by this girl, but let me tell you, this won't be the last time that you get a hurt by some girl or that life kicks you in the teeth."

"Why?" I ask, my face pointed at the ground because unlike Mother, I don't think there is an answer from up above, yet something deep inside has to ask the question.

"Why what?" he replies.

"Why would she do this to me?" I ask picking my coat and hat off the garage floor.

"Son, that's the wrong question." He flicks off a row of lights in the garage. "Ain't no sense asking why. The only question is what's next? It's a big world of hurt, get used to it."

"What do you mean?" I ask, hungering for my father's words for once in my life.

"Everybody gets beat up," he says, the lines in his face casting shadows in the dim light. "What matters isn't why you got beat up, but that you can get up, dust yourself off, and face another day. If you spend your time whining and asking why, you'll just stay knocked down."

"But how?"

"You just do," he says, and the blinding light of the obvious hits me even in the darkness. I'm not sure why the idea of unending and universally shared pain is supposed to bring me comfort, but somehow it does. The universe is right here in front of me: I know the example of my father's life, day in and day out, is the best explanation he can give. I follow in his footsteps, as he turns off the last light switch. The garage goes dark, he locks the door, and we walk, not touching but still connected, toward the house together.

Eighteen

Anything?"

"Anything," Alex repeats when I reach him the next day on the phone after school.

He sounds like hell, which is five times better than I sound. I went to bed at three and didn't crawl out from under the covers until almost noon, but Dad didn't kick the bed even once. It's like a sleepless nightmare. The image of Kylee and Sean is a splinter in my eye that no amount of tears can wash out.

"Did you see Sean at school today?" I ask.

"I saw him, but I kept my distance," Alex replies.

"You didn't say anything to him, did you?"

"Well, I don't really know much," Alex says, and sighs.

"I know only what my eyes saw, which was them together," I say. "That was enough."

"What are you going to do?" he asks. "Do you want me to do anything?"

"I want you to kill him, or me, or maybe Kylee, or maybe all three of us," I announce.

"What about rehearsal?" Alex asks, believing the band still matters and will endure.

"Go ahead without me," I say, not ready for a breakup encore. "Just practice like everything's normal. Tell Sean I'm sick, which wouldn't be a lie."

"It's not the same," Alex says.

"Buddy, it will never be the same again," I say with both grief and fury. "Just do me one favor."

"Like I said, anything, but I think you should know—"

"What?" I interrupt.

"I've known Sean a long time, and he's a good friend. He's obviously been a prick, but we have a history," Alex says, his anxiety obvious. "And I know we've got history too. But don't make me do it, please."

"Do what?"

"Choose."

I pull the phone away, shut my eyes, and bury my face into my pillow to stifle a scream. Kylee chose Sean, so why won't Alex? Can I take him siding with Sean?

"You there?" Alex asks after a few moments of dead air on the phone, which is all that is left to escape from my lungs. "Look, Bret, I'll help you, but don't make me choose."

"I understand," I tell him, though it's a lie. I left my understanding with my mom's mac and cheese back in Sean's driveway. "Just act like nothing's happened for tonight, and if you could, do me one favor, until I have a chance to talk to Kylee."

"What do you need me to do?" Alex asks slowly, his hesitation understandable.

"After practice, you guys go someplace together. Go to Venus. Just pile in the Crown Vic, so I can know that tonight he's not with her again. Just do this one thing for me."

"If it helps you, then of course," he replies.

"More than you know," I say. We hang up so I can go find Mom. I want to drive her to work—for the first time—and then drive myself to Kylee's. I'm not even sure if I want her back or if I want to show her the knife that she and Sean put in my back.

I drop Mom at Wal-Mart around four, then lie to her that I'm headed over to Alex's. How easy it must have been for Kylee to tell me she loved me, for Sean to act like my friend, for the two of them to smile to my face as they betrayed me. Mom has arranged for Dad to pick her up, so I don't need to worry about her, although whether or not she should worry about me is subject to question.

I make a rare stop at my brother, Cameron's trailer. His wife, Sandy, is home with the kids. I tell her some story about needing a certain CD, and she lets me in. She then goes back to reading some trashy tabloid while her two kids stare at the TV. Unnoticed, I liberate their libation from under the kitchen sink. While our father has taken all Twelve Steps, Cameron tries not to fall down the three in front of his trailer every weekend night when he comes home drunk. I slip the bottle of Jack Daniels into my coat, grab a CD to make the lie true, and flee the scene.

The snotsmobile is in Kylee's driveway when I make the first drive-by, gathering up my nerve. As I walk to the front door, I think about those famous astronaut words: "One small step for man . . ." But for me, each step is one huge leap as I try to walk like a man.

"Bret, how wonderful to see you!" Mrs. Edmonds says, inviting me in with open arms.

"Is Kylee home?" I ask, almost unable to hear the answer. I lose either way, yes or no.

"She's in her room, probably writing in her journal. I just love how creative she is!" she says, and starts walking toward Kylee's room. "Let me get her." Unlike in my house, where shouting is preferred to strolling even a few feet, Mrs. Edmonds disappears to summon the daughter she loves, a feeling I shared until yesterday.

"Cutie, what a surprise!" Kylee says, emerging from her bedroom with her mother. She means that in the best way, I'm sure. She looks as beautiful as ever despite her ugly actions.

"I have to do some grocery shopping, I'll be back in an hour or so," Mrs. Edmonds says, reaching for her coat. "Will you need a ride home before then?"

I answer by pointing outside. She peaks out the window, then claps her hands together. "Bret, you drove over! Congratulations."

"Well, it was Kylee's inspiration," I say, knowing only too well that truth is a double-edged sword.

"How so?" Mrs. Edmonds asks, her right hand on her chin, intently awaiting my answer.

"I followed her advice and finally did what my dad told me," I reply, eyes averted from both Edmonds women.

"I'm surprised to hear Kylee suggesting that someone listen to their parents," she says. It's probably the first mean thing ever to leave Mrs. Edmonds's lips in front of me.

"Mom, I thought you were going to the store," Kylee says in full eye-roll mode.

Her mother gives Kylee a hug and a kiss, then I get the same. She buttons her coat and is out of the door. Kylee grabs my hand, "An hour, that's enough time, nudge-nudge, wink-wink."

We're in the bedroom in ten seconds, undressed in thirty. I wonder if my five senses will detect Sean, since my sixth one did not. I'm surprised that I'm able to do this. I wonder if I'm an even better actor than Mr. Douglas thought. After we finish, at my suggestion, Kylee heads toward the shower. I tell her that I'll join her in just a moment. I tell her lies without remorse.

When I hear the shower start. I know this is my chance to strip her emotionally naked instead. My eyes dart around the crowded room. Kylee is a collector: every Harry Potter book and by-product ever created, Troll dolls, and pictures of ballet dancers. But that is what she keeps on the outside, what she hangs for show. What she writes in her purple journal is what she keeps on the inside, things she tells no one else. I walk over to the rolltop desk. The element of my surprise visit works for me—the top drawer is unlocked. I open it slowly. The water washes over Kylee's beautiful body while my blood runs cold at the ugly thought of what I will do.

As I reach into the drawer, her cell phone rings. She doesn't yell. She's not heard the phone or me sucking my breath in. I pick up the cell phone, and answer it without a word.

"Kylee?" Judas disguised as Sean says.

I wait him out in silence. The line goes dead, and I feel like joining it.

I pause, then I dial *69.

"Whadup Kylee, why didn't you answer," I hear Sean say. I hold my breath press the off button. I look at the time. It's close to 7:00, so Alex has arrived at Sean's by now. Sean believes I'm sick and they're making plans. I turn off the phone as I hear Kylee turn the water off, so I dress quickly. I drop the cell on the bed and snatch the journal from the desk on my way out of her house and her life.

After a few miles, I pull over to the side of the road. I'm just down the street from Sean's house. I put my hands on the purple journal cover and close my eyes. A few cars drive past, and I realize I'm not ready to dive into the past yet. To fight the temptation, I get out of the car and toss the journal into the Metro's messy trunk, next to the emergency tool kit. I slam the trunk hard, and it feels good. I slide back into the front seat. Inside the band rehearses; out here, I'm ready to act.

I see Sean's SUV in the driveway, and I'm thinking how much I love the sound of breaking glass. But I also know that possessions matter more to those who don't have many, than to those who have plenty. Maybe that's why Kylee meant so much to me. I think about the little happiness I've had in my life. Now it's all gone, the taste of Kylee makes me sick. I put out my last cigarette, the fourth I've smoked in an hour, then toss the unopened Jack Daniels into the backseat. My father's had the will to avoid drinking for sixteen years. I can follow his example for the next sixty minutes.

Around 8:30, about a half-hour sooner than normal, I see the lights go on outside of Sean's house. I inch up, turning off the lights and music. I hear two voices, which I assume are Alex and Sean. Moments later, I see Alex's Crown Vic leave.

After a few minutes, I park next to Sean's SUV, screening my car from one neighbor. The house on the other side is empty, as fate deals me the rare pair of aces. I know there's nothing I can do to get revenge on Sean, just like there's nothing I can do to stop Hitchings, or undo Kylee crushing me. His SUV is the most visible, available source of revenge. I'm sure his dad can replace it for him, just like Kylee replaced me with him. Sean's all about having things he's never really worked for, but for once this payback is something he's earned.

I knock on the door and ring the bell, just to be sure his mother isn't home. I imagine the scene at Venus: Alex flirts with Elizabeth while Sean does his shy-guy act. They're laughing, no doubt, but I know that my laugh here won't be the last one. I'll never get that with Sean, but this, this will have to do: I will do the best with the tools I have; I will do the worst with the tools I have. There is no answer at the door; there is only one answer available to me.

I open the trunk, then hunt through the crowded toolbox. I grab a handful of nails, some long, some short, some bent, some straight, and then take hold of the dull, thick hammer. Lining the nails like bullets, I remember telling my mom and Principal Morgan and the rest that I didn't condone the violence at Columbine. That I would never be capable of such behavior myself. And it's true. Driving the nails into each tire, two or three swings deep into the tread until I hit steel, I know I'm killing something that's already dead. I know I'm doing something wrong, so I use a hammer.

Sean's too carefree to lock the car, so I open the driver's-side door and pop the hood. I begin driving nails through every hose. An experienced pro now, I have no trouble finding the oil filter, which is where I drive the final nail home before I drive myself home.

As I leave, I drive by Hitchings's house, and I wish I was like those shrewd, soulless criminals you see on TV. I would figure out a way to pin this on him, and kill two vultures with one Stone Cold–inspired move. But Hitchings will have to wait until I am physically stronger, or morally weaker. I'm certain this isn't over with Sean, but I don't care and I won't hear, since I never plan to speak to him or Kylee again.

I never want to hear Kylee's voice, but I still want to know her heart. I want to know how she could break mine so easily. I try to imagine the scene when Sean arrives home, but already the passion of payback has evaporated. There's no laughter, first or last.

When I get home, I open the trunk and pull out Kylee's journal. After exchanging forced pleasantries with Mom, I lock myself in my room, ready to learn how Kylee exchanged me for Sean. As I open up the pages to Kylee's journal, I hope that it'll provide the answer to the only question that really matters. I don't care about when or where or even how often. In the pages of Kylee's journal, I seek an answer to the question that Father has warned me never to ask: why?

Nineteen

September 6

Senior year, finally. My last year in Flint under the spell of the ShadowCaster. I'm so glad I've hooked up with Bret. He lets me be the light in his life. If I can keep him happy (nudge-nudge), then he'll keep me even happier (wink-wink). I love falling in love! I'm sorry about Chad. I'll cut him loose now that Bret and are tight. I'm glad Bret came along, so I didn't have to feel alone for even one day, and it's not like Chad really loved me, anyway. Bret's the sweetest guy in the world. He wants to be with me so much; feeling is mutual. I hope my parents hate him. He's a year younger than me (even younger than his age in many ways), but that's okay since I'm out of here next year.

September 7

Met Sean Dupont, one of Bret's pals yesterday. There's something about him. He's shy, but

seems self-confident. Interesting mix, kind of
like me.

October 8

I told Bret I loved him. If I can just keep us out of
the house and away from my parents, then I won't
have to compete for his attention. Next week, I'm
going to see Bret's band debut. It'll be exciting, but
I'm jealous. I would LOVE to have people love what I
do so I can suck in that applause. I wish I could get
onstage (something other than a dance recital with
no one in the audience but parents). My parents
wanted to go see Bret's band, but I blew them off. If
they came, the evening would be about them, not me.

October 16

What an amazing night. I was worried for Bret, and
scared that his band wouldn't be any good, but wow!
He's charismatic when he sings. After the show, Bret
and Alex just took off, something about some rock.
So Sean gave me a ride. If Bret ever grows up, he'll
be able to drive us places. Sean's really good-
looking, but kind of shy so it was fun to flirt with him
a little. I helped them paint the rock with the name of
their band. My 18th bday is coming up and I told Bret
it would be cool to see my name up there. Bret's so

loving, not that he's said that word to me yet. I've heard them before, from Chad, but this time love will last.

October 17

Bad scene at this party last night where Bret was hassled by this asshole named Hitchings. Thank God, Sean was there to help, since I don't think Bret knew what to do.

November 4

I love Bret to death, but I never see him. When we met this summer, we talked all the time and he was like so into me. I got all his attention, but now he is so busy with plays, his band, his lame job, so now I don't see him much. I'm going over tonight to drive him to his play for opening night (I wonder if Sean's going?). I always have to drive because he's so immature, acting like he's ten years old and pouting about this thing with his dad. He's real gutless sometimes about standing up to people like Hitchings or letting his dad boss him around.

November 18

Sean called the other day looking for Bret. He wasn't here, but Sean and I talked for a long time. He's really smart and pretty funny. He kept telling me how lucky Bret was to have a beautiful girlfriend like me. It would be nice if Bret remembered anymore to say once in a while that I was beautiful, like he did last August. I love Bret, but it just isn't the same as B4. I'm trying to tell him I need more, but he's not listening.

November 19

Bret is always going on about how different he is from other people, but when it comes right down to it, once you take away all his "look," he's more or less like every other guy I've been with, except for that Monster in his pants, which I don't like putting in my mouth (GAG). He's whiny sometimes too: he wants to dress and talk the way he wants but isn't secure enough to deal with people who make fun of him. He's got a lot of growing up to do.

November 26

So I turned eighteen years old yesterday and I guess I should be all happy, but…Bret, I know that he tries, but chocolate and cigarettes? It's like I'm in prison or something! He wrote me this romantic letter (it's clipped in), and he did this really nice thing with a Wizard of Oz poster—he still remembers that I was wearing my ruby red slippers the first time we kissed. Alex didn't get me anything, which doesn't surprise me one iota, since he doesn't care about anything that doesn't have to do with how great and wonderful and perfect Alex is. The nicest gift I got was from Sean: twelve red roses and the lyrics to "Tiny Dancer," this old Elton John song. I thought about him in the shower (Sean, not Elton!) Gotta Bmorecareful; don't want to hurt Bret, but Sean is obviously interested.

December 9

Sean called again, this time just to talk. He said if my dance group ever needed a drummer, to call him (I've got his cell now). Followed his call with a long shower.

December 22

With Bret's schedule and with my parents acting like the Royalty of Flint, this has been such a crazy month. They told me the other day that since I was 18, it was OK if Bret wanted to stay overnight, so we wouldn't have to drive him home with the weather getting bad. Why can't I just have normal parents? My body, and what I do with it, that's about all I have that's mine to do with what I please when I please and nothing to do with them.

December 24

Sean sent me flowers again, this time for Xmas, and he also sent them for Hanukkah and Ramadan, he said just to cover all the bases. My question to him: What about Kwanza??? I can't stop thinking about him. It's just like Bret last summer when I was going out with that bore Chad. Sean pays so much attention to me, just like Bret used to. Don't know what to do. I'm going to see Sean next Monday night and see what happens.

December 25

Sean called to wish me a merry Xmas. We talk most every day now. He doesn't think that Bret knows, which is good because Bret is such a sweetie and I think he loves me (but would it kill him just to say it one time???) and I don't want to hurt him. I can't talk to my mom about this (so what else is NEW???) because she thinks he's so good. They really like Bret's working-class roots, they say. (Not they have ever even met his parents, which is so typical: say one thing, do another. Such posers.) Sean says that I should start singing with the band and that he'll quit the band if they don't let me up onstage where I belong. I know that Bret wouldn't let me do that. He's married to Alex, and Alex hates me out of jealousy.

December 26

Bret came over tonight and it was the usual fiasco.
He told my parents about the thing at school with his
speech (his life is just so interesting to my parents)
and they both got so all involved (big surprise). My
mother wants to take over the whole thing. And they
just love him so much I wish they'd just adopt him
and get it over with. <u>I don't know what I'm going to
do. I wish Bret would break up with me.</u> I'll try being
a bitch (I guess being fatandugly isn't enuff) because I
don't want to hurt Bret, but I'm falling in love with
Sean. Bret's done nothing wrong, but I can't really
control this thing with Sean. I'm watching the band
rehearse now because I don't have anything better to
do and it's about the only time that Bret has time for
me anymore. On the way over, we have this weird talk
and Bret asks me to kill him if he ever gets normal. I
resist the urge to kill him on the spot, since it would
crush him to know that even normal people color
their hair and have father issues. Which is ironic,
because although I love Bret, especially after the real
gift he gave me, I wish he was dead. Not because I
hate him, but because he is such a sweetie and I just
know that he's going to get hurt, so if he would just
break up with me now that would be best for me, him,
and Sean. Sean thinks Alex is such a joke and jerk-off

and we now call him Wordboy when he's not around, but still Sean likes to be in the band, feels kind of sorry for Alex, since they've known each other for so long. But mostly Sean likes to see me. Alex is giving him such a hard time. The band wouldn't even be together if not for Sean, since he gives them a place to practice, pays for everything, etc. I can't stand how they hassle Sean, when he's Santa to them.

December 27

Big fight last night, so I left in a huff, leaving U behind. I drove around for a while and just thought about stuff. I asked myself a question and the question was this: What do I want? Who wants me more? I know the answer. I asked it last August, but I guess things change. It's nothing Bret did or even Sean; it just happened. I can't control what my heart wants. I waited an hour before I drove back to Sean's and I saw that POS car that Alex drives was gone. I knocked on the door with the excuse to pick U, dearest diary, up, but that's not what I wanted to pick up. All Sean needed was alcoholic inspiration it seemed.

December 28

Sean's so great. He tells me how he would do anything for me and how he was breaking up his band for me.

nailed

I feel bad about hurting Bret and should probably break up with him now, but I'm still not totally sure Sean is the one, and I can't face being without someone.

January 1

New year and I don't have big resolutions, just one decision: Sean or Bret? I don't know how much longer I can sneak around before Bret finds out. I feel so lousy about Bret. Decisions!!!!

February 12

Earlier tonight, while Bret was watching wrestling, I was rolling around with Sean on our normal Monday night date. Unlike Bret, Sean doesn't pick TV over me. I decided to do the deed for Sean (GAG). I want to keep him happy so he doesn't fall out of love with me like Bret did. It is not like I wanted any of this to happen, like with Chad. I don't want to hurt Bret, but I'm afraid my heart has made the decision for me.

Twenty

My heart has made the decision for me."

I try to sleep, but I'm even a failure at that. Sometime around 4:00 a.m., an hour before Dad rises to start his day, I realize that I need to start my work. I'm sure that Sean and Kylee will have spoken and compared notes: the missing journal, the silent cell phone call, and my infantile and excellent act of vengeance on one of Sean's possessions, which is hardly prized.

I open the journal again. It's like an auto accident I can't look away from as I rubberneck on Kylee's betrayal, Sean's deceitfulness, and my heart breaking. As I reread certain entries, each line of black ink slices my heart into ever-smaller pieces, with her calling me "gutless," the sword on which I'm impaled and impaired.

I realize that Sean read these same words, no doubt the night after Christmas when she left the journal at his house. I thought Sean and I were fighting about singing that night; I was off-key on that one. It explains so much, from things about me Sean knew (I'll never forget him saying, "That monster you have between your legs") to things that Kylee thought but never chose to share with me. Sean knew what she was thinking and feeling. He had the answers to the exam.

I creep from my bedroom and confiscate Dad's extra keys from their hiding place in the top drawer in the kitchen. Bundling up, I go out to the garage and start my search. My dad has all the cabinets labeled and locked, except the one with his rifles, which is unmarked and double-locked. I flash a glance at the first lock but abandon the idea. "I'm not like Eric and Dylan," I recall telling Mom in Morgan's office. Pulling a trigger wouldn't get Kylee back in my life, press out images of Sean from my mind, or get this splinter out of my eye.

I look at the journal one final time and find the entry from October ("*My 18th bday is coming up and I told Bret it would be cool to see my name up there*") and think about delivering an early Valentine's Day present, announcing my hurt and heartbreak on the Rock, but I reject it. Besides, whatever I do there is temporary, just another prop. Just like me.

I back the Metro out of the driveway, the journal beside me, and me beside myself. I arrive at the Grand Trunk Railroad overpass as the sun is just peeking up. Like Dad, I'm starting work before sunrise. Parking in front of my *Bret Lives Kylee* declaration, I climb out of the car. I'm ready to again follow my dad's life lesson as I retrieve the hammer from the trunk of the car.

I smash the hammer into the concrete embankment, each strike an exclamation point. My heart is closed for repairs, which I'm making one hammer blow at a time. I bring the hammer down hard and fast. I bring it down again, the noise loud enough to wake the dead, which is what Kylee is to me now. Inch by inch, letter by letter, I smash the hammer into the wall.

Again and again.

As my sweat mixes with the dust, I know it isn't enough. The splinter remains. I inspect my work and expect the fury to dissipate, but this isn't, as Kylee would say, all about me.

There's a 24/7 Walgreen's drugstore a couple blocks away. I walk in, feeling rich with the money from Jellybean still in my pocket. I buy a Polaroid camera and some film and return to the Grand Trunk crossing for the last act.

Photographing my handiwork from every angle up close and far away, I want Kylee to see every available perspective, just as I've read her perspective on me, on Sean, on Alex (should I tell him?), and even on her own parents. They are so cool and she's so wrong, but what was it that my mom said? Consider the source. There's just enough light for this cheap little Polaroid camera to do its work and document what I've done and what they've done to me.

I head across town to Kylee's house, but the snotsmobile isn't there. I think about leaving the journal and the pictures in the door, but I don't want to take the chance of her parents finding them. By now, school is starting and Kylee needs to learn her lesson.

I head next over to Central and search the parking lot. Kylee is wrong about Chad Lake: she's the one who is a puddle; shallow but casting a great reflection. I find her car, but it's locked. I'd like to grab my trusty hammer and hear the sound of breaking glass, but such an act would only hurt her parents. Like me, they are fatalities of Kylee's unfaithfulness. I go into the trunk and get out the flexi-stick, an emergency tool for unlocking a car door; yet another emergency my dad has prepared me for.

I use the stick to pop open the passenger door of the snotsmobile. I sit in the seat I used to occupy and take in the smell of clove cigarettes. I put the journal on the dashboard and place within it two Polaroids.

I sit in the snotsmobile for the last time, scrunch my eyes together, and try to imagine the scene of Kylee coming out to her car. She'll be talking to Sean on her cell. I wonder what other phone numbers are in there? Poor son of a bitch Sean doesn't get it: he's just the next big thing. For the rest of my life, I want to run ten feet in front of Kylee with a sign warning every guy away, but I guess they'll have to learn for themselves the hard way. Like I did.

I picture her opening up the journal, confused as to how it got there, but even more grateful that it was returned. I have thoughts of burning it, but then I remember *The Princess Bride*, another movie like *Monty Python and the Holy Grail* that Kylee and I would act out because we both knew the dialogue so well. Rather than killing his enemy after he backs down from a duel, the protagonist, Wesley, lets his enemy live. Not because Wesley is merciful, but because he isn't. He wants him to forever remember his cowardice. I want Kylee to forever remember her unfaithfulness. I want Kylee to keep a record of her betrayal. I'd like to burn these words; instead, I hope they burn into her memory.

As she closes the journal, I wonder if she'll feel anything or even shed a tear? I wonder how she'll react when she touches the white frames of the Polaroids, when she sees the desecration of my Christmas gift, shattered like my spirit. I have obliterated her name from my history, and all that's left is in the picture and all that she needs to know:

BRET LIVES

Twenty-one

 quit."

I throw the *Bye Bye Birdie* script at Mr. Douglas with an anger and energy I wasn't capable of until this past week. I'm being dramatic, but this isn't acting. This is the real deal.

"Take five!" Mr. Douglas shouts at the stage, where I'm supposed to be with the other members of the cast. "No, wait, work on that scene on your own—try it at half speed, slow it down, let the words have time to breathe."

Although his attention is divided, he's always willing to give me 100 percent. "Sorry," I offer sheepishly.

"No. You do not quit. I won't accept that," Mr. Douglas calmly replies.

"I can't do it. I can't do anything," I say, sitting down next to him in the third row. It's our first rehearsal with the band, most of them from the school's jazz ensemble, so it's a full house. But I'm ready to fold my hand.

"Bret, give me about three minutes to work out this scene, then let's you and me go into my office and talk," Mr. Douglas says, tilting his head toward the stage. I was there once, thinking that theater was just about memorizing your lines word for word.

Thanks to Mr. Douglas, I learned that there's more to it than that. Theater is about building a character, and falling in love is the easiest way to lose it, as Kylee, Sean, and I have all proved.

I nod in thanks and then go toward his office in the back of the theater, its door always unlocked. Before I disappear backstage, I look at Mr. D. sitting with his clipboard resting in his lap, red thermos of coffee next to him. He looks like all of the other teachers at school, with his short hair and casually conservative style of dress. You look at him from the outside and he looks normal, but it's not the costume, it's the character that counts.

"Hey, Bret, how's it going?" It's Will Kennedy, from my English class.

"Fine," I mutter. I barely have the energy to speak to my family and friends, let alone classroom acquaintances like Will.

"This theater stuff is a lot of fun," he says, all smiles. "I'm doing drums for this show."

"Really?" I pretend to care about Will, about theater, about anything.

"I'd be scared to death to be onstage like you," Will says.

"Thanks." I again mumble; why should I speak clearly when my life is chaos?

"Bret, you're really good in this show," Will adds. I hear the sound of my own name and it sounds odd. I don't really think I'll ever be Bret again. No matter that I hammered Kylee from the stone so that only "Bret Lives." It's a lie. I'm not Bret and I'm barely alive. No way I can do the part Mr. Douglas cast me for in *Bye Bye Birdie*. I've come here today to tell him I'm quitting. I'm a good actor, but I can't pull off the role of a singer who all the girls adore.

"Maybe, but then, I can't play drums or play baseball like you can, Will."

"That's just having strong arms," Will says, almost ashamed to be acknowledged.

"It's more than that," I say, realizing Alex was wrong: Will's just like us, trying to figure it out the best he can. We were prejudging him, as others did to us.

"See you in class tomorrow," I say to Will, noticing Mr. Douglas walking past me. Before I enter his office I stifle a yawn, thanks to another sleepless night, as visions of Kylee's plum lips danced through my head.

I sit down in Mr. D.'s tiny office, which is as cluttered and messy as Dad's garage is organized and clean, and the contrast with Principal Morgan's office could not be starker. Morgan's office is full photos of football teams staring blankly at the camera, whereas Mr. D.'s office is lined with photos of laughing students. Going from Morgan's office, or even Mold King Cold's classroom, into this sanctuary was a trip through the Twilight Zone.

"So what's this about quitting?" Mr. Douglas asks, pouring himself another steaming hot cup of coffee from his ever-present red thermos, licking the lid. It's a disgusting habit, but like the Greek tragic heroes Mr. D. taught us about, all great men have a flaw.

"I can't do it, that's all," I say. He thinks about that for a moment, knowing I'm only giving him the line and not the motivation. I look at the red thermos and remember something Alex, Sean, and I did last year. We got Mom to drive the three of us around to every thrift store in Flint so we could buy as many red thermoses as we could find. On the day of the final test in Mr. D.'s class, he looked out into the room, and there were all of his students in Theater II, each with their own red thermos. His face turned red with embarrassment, then filled with a huge smile. He wasn't angry, immediately understanding that it wasn't a taunt, it was a tribute.

"I think you owe me an explanation," he says. I know there's a debt to be paid for him sticking up for me in Morgan's office, but I don't want to get into it. I just don't want to dump my crap on him and cover him in my stink.

"I can't play the part," I reply.

"Okay, then maybe another part. I could recast the play," he says.

I'm not thinking about the play, I'm thinking about my life. Kylee recast her life, changing the person playing the role of the boyfriend. Sean's now in my place in her heart, bed, and life. I'm still sorting out my anger, wondering which of these substitutions hurts the most.

"That's not it, I just can't do it. I want to quit," I repeat, eyes studying the floor.

"You're not a quitter," he reminds me. "Like wrestling. You didn't quit that."

"I guess," I say with a shrug. It was the worst three months of my life, but he's right, I didn't quit because everyone, including Dad, thought I would. Instead, I took the hard road.

"I don't want you to give up. You're a great talent. I've been doing this for fifteen years, so trust me on this. You're very good," he says, then sips his coffee. "Is this because of the stuff going on between you and Mr. Morgan? If it is, I could—"

"Morgan hates me," I say, thinking how he's not the only one.

"Why do you say that, Bret?"

"The fact that he suspended me twice."

"Which he should have," he says forcefully. "What Coach King said to you wasn't right, but what you said was just as wrong. If you would have said that to me, you would have faced the same result."

I nod, trying to hide my eyes.

"The concert? I would have done the same," he adds, driving yet another knife deeper and harder into my back.

"But they wouldn't let us play inside and we wanted to—" I start to explain.

"Bret, what makes the plays we do here work? I mean, when they're really good? Is it because everybody just says the lines they want and ignores the other characters?"

"No, it isn't," I admit.

"It works when people do their parts. When they do what's needed for the greater good of the play and not just for themselves," he says. "If every student did exactly what he or she wanted, you know what we'd have at this school? Chaos. And nobody wants that, right?"

"I'm sorry," I reply, caught like a fly in my web of Alex-like egomania.

"Well, I'll let you drop the lead, but I still want you in the play."

I shake my head vigorously, exaggerated in a way that would be over the top even from the distance of the stage. It's not just that I don't want to be in a play. I want to be left alone.

"You can't quit. You've got to stay connected, especially now," he says. I wonder what he means and what he knows. Do teachers talk about their students? Does he know about Kylee and Sean? Why should he know when I didn't until the other night?

"Okay, you win, Mr. D.," I say, too tired to argue, especially with someone so right.

"Good, but the only part I can change out is the role of Hugo

Peabody. You'll like it because you get to do a lot of physical comedy. You could probably even work in some wrestling falls."

"What's his part again?" I ask, struggling to get reconnected.

"His character is the jilted boyfriend."

"Perfect!" Comedy pins tragedy's shoulders to the mat.

Twenty-two

March 21, Junior Year

More coffee?"

"No thanks, Elizabeth," I say without looking up, not wanting to gaze into her retro-glasses. I'm waiting with Alex at Venus for her shift to end and my life to begin again.

"Sean wants to talk to you," Alex says once Elizabeth heads away from the table.

"Alex, you need to tell him."

"Look, I can't get in the middle of this!" Alex snaps, fueled by frustration.

"That's fine, because there's nothing for you to be in the middle of," I reply.

"What about the band?" Alex asks, since we've not rehearsed in over a month.

"I'm going to have to ask you to do something that you don't want to do."

"What's that?"

"Choose," I tell him as I watch his face fall.

"God, Bret, don't make me."

"You can be friends with Sean if you still want, it's your life. But as far as the band, I won't be in it if he is. I don't ever want to see Sean again, period," I say, amazed at how certain I seem about the bottom line, but there's no Stone Cold Austin homage here. This is me.

"He says you can work something out about what you did to his ride," Alex informs me.

"I don't have anything to work out because I didn't do anything."

"Don't lie to me," Alex says. "And don't ever use me like that again."

"Feels pretty shitty to get used and lied to, doesn't it?" I vent, angry at Alex, angry at myself, angry at the world, and angriest at a world without Kylee.

"Do this for me, you owe me," Alex says softly.

"How do I owe you?" I ask.

"I didn't know it at the time, but I did help you wreck Sean's SUV by bringing him here and getting him out of the house like you asked," Alex replies with force.

Part of me wants to tell Alex how much Kylee dislikes him, just to poison the air around Sean. All my anger is turned back, at least for today, against Sean. Why would I want to hurt Kylee? I loved her, although that verb remains tense as I avoid the temptation to call her and plead my case. Every time the phone rings, I go from hope to humility, as I realize it's not her calling to say, "I'm sorry, cutie, come back." Looking at lovely Elizabeth, with her short, spiky bright red hair, set off by the dull blue of the Venus waitress polo shirt, I'm lonelier than ever.

Alex pauses for forever. "Where are you and I going to rehearse now?" he asks.

"I'll figure that out, you start writing new songs," I say, feeling reconnected.

"And finding us a new drummer," Alex adds.

"How about Will Kennedy?" I say, almost hoping he didn't hear me.

"Are you crazy? He's jazz band," Alex replies with disgust. "He can't play my songs."

"Why don't we give him a chance?" I counter.

"And he's a jock, right?" Alex raves on. "Plays baseball or something, right?"

"But he's doing the band for *Bye Bye Birdie* and he seems okay."

"Who are you again?" Alex says, then laughs. "A jazz-band jock, wow."

I take a deep breath, then take the plunge. "It gets worse before it gets better."

"What are you talking about?" he asks, as Elizabeth joins us at the table. Following a quick kiss, she puts her tired feet on Alex's lap for him to rub.

"We need to get a drummer because I got us a gig in a couple of months," I say.

"Finally, I get to see you play," Elizabeth says dramatically, then kisses Alex's hand.

"Where?" Alex asks.

"I was talking to Becca Levy. She's in my English class and is planning the prom—"

"The prom!" Alex yells, but I notice that Elizabeth has this twisted grin on her face.

"That's perfect," Elizabeth says to my surprise. She swings her long legs under the table, and leans forward. "Don't you see?"

"See what?" Alex asks.

"Everybody will be all dressed up, and you'll punk 'em," Elizabeth says, looking older and sounding wiser than her eighteen years. She's a tough one: it took Alex over a month to get her to agree to a date, then another month before he told her he was only in high school.

"We'll shove our songs up their tight white asses," I say. "This will be our payback."

"No way Morgan will allow this," Alex says.

"Look, Becca says it's no problem and—" I start to explain.

"I see what this is about. You and Becca?" he says with smugness in his voice and his studded eyebrow raised in disbelief.

"This isn't about Becca," I reply.

"We'll need a warm-up gig," he says, obviously on board, if appalled.

"Let's do something at the *Birdie* cast party. Will's in the band for the show, so—"

"Baseball pals, proms, you're turning into a regular high school hero," Alex shoots back. "Next thing you'll be running for student council, making speeches, and waving the flag."

"Listen, Alex, I won't be part of the problem by staying silent," I say, my mind racing back to the warmth of the Edmonds dinner table. "I'm part of the solution."

"Maybe that's your wrestling name: Bret the Problem Solver," Alex jokes, as the three of us head off into the night: Alex and Elizabeth into each other's arms, and me to my misery.

Almost as soon as they drop me off and I walk in the door, I hear the phone ringing. Before I can answer, Robin rushes to it. She's on the phone for a while, before she yells with a middle-school-girl giggle, "Bret, it's Becca."

"Becca Levy?" I shout back. If my heart still functioned, it might have skipped a beat at this news. I pick up the phone in the living room.

"Hello, Bret. It's Kylee. I'm sorry I lied to your sister, but I have to talk to you."

I want to scream, but I have no voice. Instead, I stare into the telephone receiver.

"Don't hang up! Please, let's talk. I'm so sorry," she says.

"We don't have anything to talk about," I spit out. But I can't slam the receiver down.

"Cutie, I'm so sorry about everything," she says, just like her voice in my dreams.

"Does Sean know you're calling me?" I snap back.

"This isn't about Sean, this is about us," Kylee says, not about to be distracted by my bitterness. "There is no Sean. That's over. That was a mistake, you have to forgive me."

"I don't want to talk to you," I lie.

"You have to talk with me. Cutie, I miss you so much. About Sean—let me explain."

"I've read your explanation," I remind her, the blackness of the ink still chills me.

"I know, I'm sorry about what I wrote, what I did. I wish I could take it all back," she says, I think, because tears are drowning out her final words. "I want to make things right."

"Where are you?" I ask, letting my heart bully my head.

"I'm at home, I'm all alone and scared. Please come over." Kylee sounds as lonely and forlorn as anyone in the world, except perhaps for me. "I don't know what I'm going to do. I'm so sorry that I hurt you, Bret. I'm sorry that I messed up everything. I can't take it anymore."

"What are you talking about?"

"It hurts too much, Bret, it hurts too much," she whispers. "I don't want to live anymore!"

"Kylee, what are you—?" The phone goes dead, then I race for the door.

I grab the car keys, but running out the door, I realize that Mom took the Metro tonight. I see the light on, as always, in the garage. Gasping for breath, I go inside, but Dad is nowhere to be found. His Camaro is there though, and I know where he keeps the keys.

"Bret, what's going on?" Dad says, startling me when he steps into the garage.

"I need to borrow your truck tonight." I ask, but don't beg.

"I don't think so," he chuckles, reaching for a Marlboro.

"Then what about—?" I glance at the Camaro.

"Don't even think about it." The humor and color drain immediately from his face.

"Then can you give me a ride?" I ask, willing to admit my dependence in my desperation.

He lights the smoke. "Where to?"

"Kylee's," I say coldly.

He shakes his head, a gesture I don't see as much since our breakthrough night when I changed the oil in Mom's Metro. "Bad idea, son."

I don't have time for explanations or excuses. "I need to see her."

He slams the hood of the pickup down and wipes the grease off his hand. "How long?"

"Just drop me there. I'll get back myself," I say.

Another head shake. "If you go back, you'll stay back, know what I mean?"

"I think so," I admit, tugging on my ponytail, now lacking color. When Kylee left my world, she took part of me with her. I want it back. I want her back. I want the old Bret back.

As he climbs into the cab, there's another head shake, smoke leaving his lungs, a knowing smile dawning on his face, all followed by a question: "Still doing things the hard way, huh?"

"Now what?" I ask, nearly an hour later, in bed with Kylee. We let our bodies speak, for there are no words, doubts, or regrets as Kylee is mine again above all else. I don't want to talk about why or when or how often. There's no taking her back, since she never ever left my heart.

"I didn't want to live without you, cutie, it hurt that much," Kylee says, explaining away her exaggerated excuse to get me in her house and bed again. She leans over to kiss me, and I run my hands up and down the length of her body. She told me the second I walked through the door that she was sorry, that things with Sean were over, and that she wanted me again. Our bodies fit back together like two separated pieces of a jigsaw puzzle.

"Kylee, I've missed you so much."

"Bret, I'm so sorry," Kylee says, her voice wavering on waves of emotion.

"Have you missed me?" A positive answer will wash away all my negative thoughts.

"More than I could ever tell you or show you," she continues. "I'm sorry about Sean. I didn't want to hurt you, but I thought you didn't love me anymore."

"It's okay," I reassure her, deciding that forgiving her betrayal beats out being without her.

"I had to see you again," Kylee says, her eyes starting to mist. "It just happened, but it won't happen again. I can't be apart from you. I know I'm not strong enough to stay away."

"Not like me," I tease and show off my almost nonexistent biceps, allowing a light laughter to illuminate the darkness that had invaded our lives. I pump my arms, even though I have nothing to flex other than my morals. I know I look ridiculous; that's the real joke.

Kylee laughs, puts her hand back around my neck, and pulls on my ponytail. "Wrong muscles, cutie," she says with a naughty giggle. When she laughs, I know that cracking Kylee up is like crack. I'm a Kylee Edmonds addict getting his fix and fixing our broken hearts.

Twenty-three

Will's just another jock. Doesn't that bother you?"

"He's a drummer and that's what we need," I counter. We're sitting outside on the porch in a light spring rain before playing a set with Will at the *Bye Bye Birdie* cast party at his house.

"We need a good drummer, not some jazzbone," Alex says.

"Why don't we just use a drum machine then?" I ask, avoiding Alex's glare.

"No, there'll be no drum machines in my band," Alex says, firm and final.

"But a drum machine is always on time, doesn't drink, and doesn't steal your girlfriend," I say, breaking the tension, and handing the shared smoke back to Alex.

"Let's see how he does tonight," Alex says, as he burns a small hole in his *Weekly World News* "Bat Child Found in Cave" T-shirt, then leaves me alone on the porch to finish off the smoke and gear myself up to take the makeshift basement stage in moments.

Other than rehearsing, I don't see much of Alex anymore since Kylee and I got back together. I've also vowed to not spend so much time at her house with her parents. Her folks are happy that I'm back in the picture, even if Kylee wants to ease us out of her family portrait. Alex is happy that I'm not this huge hurricane of hurt anymore, but he hasn't forgiven Kylee. I'm not sure if he's angrier at her for breaking my heart or busting up his band. I've forgiven but not forgotten, and neither has Sean, who is now the one going out of his way to avoid me at school. He's even hanging around Hitchings, probably more to taunt Alex and me than from true friendship. It's a mixed group at the party, since Will straddles both camps, so I'm worried Hitchings might bully his way into the party as he did the last one at Will's house.

I don't know Will that well yet, but he seems like an interesting guy. He uses his strong drummer arms to hurl fastballs every spring, but he also plays in a jazz band and wants to try acting. He's one of these guys that everybody likes, but he's not a drone normal. He manages to avoid the smackdown by not sticking out too much, yet he can still be himself. I admire that.

I'm trying to get better in that regard too. I see Mrs. Pfeil every week. She's good at listening, like Mom, and she protects me from the hateful actions of Hitchings, the harsh actions of Morgan, and the attention-loving antics of Bret Hendricks. Mr. Douglas has been great too. He keeps telling me, "Put it in perspective, decide what's important." I don't see the big picture a lot, sometimes just a small fragment, like the thing with Dad and the oil change. I didn't lose anything by giving in. I gained the rights to the Metro, with the added and unexpected bonus of earning a little respect from my dad, which I had thought was an impossible equation.

I pull on my once-again violet-tipped ponytail, and in doing so I flash back to the first time that Kylee and I kissed. It was outside at a party like this one. I was so infatuated with her; she doesn't get that the longer I know her, the deeper my fascination with her grows. It isn't just about attention; it's about intention. She's everything I've ever wanted.

I hear Will laying down the drumbeat, then Alex fills it in with a fury of feedback. I come in from the rain, grind out the butt on the porch stairs, then start toward the basement to make a big entrance with my fedora firmly atop my head, my bass, and a microphone already onstage for me, and Kylee dancing once again before my eyes up front.

Alex frowns as he fingers the frets on the Gibson, unwilling to hide his disappointment over the fact that since Will is new, the six songs we're doing are all covers. We're a little sloppy, but even still, following Kylee's lead, positive dancemania has broken out on the basement floor. I call for the last song and ask Kylee, clad in her now cutoff Emma Goldman red T-shirt and denim shorts over pink fishnets, to join us onstage as a guest dancer. We've got no spotlight, but my smile is large enough to light the stage.

My smile and the music fades as darkness descends down the stairs. It's Sean, with Hitchings and his bullyboy pal Jack Bison, in tow. Alex turns up the volume, but it's no use. They start heckling us, heaving their bodies toward our stage. Will puts down his sticks, moving over toward Sean and Hitchings. He's trying to talk to them, jock on jock, but Sean keeps cackling, like a hyena, and finally Will goes upstairs, I hope to dial 911.

Alex keeps playing, but looking at the alcohol-infused anger in the eyes of Sean, Hitchings, and Bison, I decide to surrender the stage.

"Look, Sean, I don't want any trouble," I say, taking a step backward.

"Pussy!" Hitchings slurs. "Maybe you ain't no faggot, but you're still a pussy."

I let it pass, because I have no other option. I look toward the crowd, and give a deep bow, throwing kisses. "Thank you, thank you very much. We're leaving the building!"

"Fuck you very much," Hitchings says, knocking the fedora off of my head. Sean staggers past me, not saying a word. He picks up Will's drumsticks and starts churning out a beat.

I bend down to pick up my hat, but Hitchings stomps it. "Just try and take it," he says.

I move away, but in doing so I bump into Bison, who bounces me back toward Hitchings, who pushes me out of his way. Alex sets his guitar down, getting it ready for the case, but Bison picks it up. Alex says something, but Bison pushes him aside. Bison starts wildly grinding on Alex's Gibson, as Sean drums a demon dance, and Hitchings screeches into the mic he's strangling. En masse, our audience moves upstairs, away from the noise. As the room clears, I spot Kylee alone in the corner, standing still, looking small, afraid, and lost. Like I feel now.

"Pussy!" Hitchings keeps shouting, pointing at me. He's got my hat on his thick head, and his hand on his thin crotch, which he keeps thrusting toward Kylee, but I'm helpless to stop this humiliation. Kylee starts to cry, while Alex stares helplessly as Bison scrapes sounds from his favorite guitar. Alex looks to me for help, but I have nothing to offer but fear and loathing.

Realizing everyone has left and there's no audience for their asshole antics, the clatter stops after a few minutes. Sean climbs out from behind the drums and comes over toward me. He jabs one of the drumsticks into the middle of my chest, not to injure but to intimidate.

"This isn't over, Bret," Sean says, the smell of Jack Daniels thick on his breath. "We used to be friends. We can work this out, right?"

"I don't want any trouble," I say as calmly as possible.

"I don't want any trouble, either," he says, and then points with his drumsticks in Kylee's direction, who remains frozen in the corner of the room. "You know what I do want?"

Before I can answer, he leans into me. The whiskey stench is strong and sickening. He pulls me so tight that he's almost whispering in my ear. "I want Kylee back."

"Sean, just let it go," I respond firmly. "Let's just forget all of this and—"

"She wants to come back to me, she told me, but she doesn't want to hurt you again. She told me she feels sorry for you, and so do I," Sean says, as he releases me from his clutches.

"You lie," I say, remembering Austin's motto of DTA: Don't Trust Anyone.

"Let me have her back," Sean slurs. "And we can forget about what you owe me for my ride. Be honest with yourself, Bret, you know it'll happen sooner or later."

"I'd rather be dead!" I protest, meaning every word: life without Kylee isn't really living at all. I look over again at Kylee, knowing that this and a million more hurts are worth her love.

"Fine, then my pop is gonna sue your white-trash ass for what you did to my ride!"

"You have no idea the damage you caused me," I tell Sean as calmly as possible.

He gives a slow motion shrug. "You know that I do, because she broke my heart too."

"Look, Sean, this is over," I say, turning to leave, my hand outstretched, beckoning Kylee to meet me at the door. Hitchings and Bison are nowhere to be seen.

"Be a tough guy!" Sean shouts after me. "My dad's a lawyer, and we'll take everything!"

"Sean, that's not going to happen, because I don't have anything," I remind him.

"We'll take your house."

"Do whatever you have to do," I say over my shoulder.

"And your mom's crappy car," he says, as I start up the stairs.

I don't turn around, instead I surround Kylee's small hand in my mine.

He's screaming now, but there's no need because I hear the next thing he says loud and clear: "And we'll take your dad's Camaro!"

"He's lying to you, Bret," Kylee says as I drive us away from the party.

"He said that you still want to be with him," I say, repeating Sean's taunt.

"He's fooling himself," Kylee says. "I'm with you. I love you."

"Then, why did—"

"He's angry. He's used to getting his way, that's all," she says indifferently.

"How can you be so sure?" I ask.

"I know him," she reassures me.

I bite my lip and ball my fist, but my internal editor lets one slip past. "Intimately."

"What does that mean?" she says, pulling away from me.

"What do you think it means?" I ask, reaching toward her. "Sorry, let's not fight."

"Sean's a good person, you know that."

I slow the car down, hoping my racing pulse will do the same. "He used to be."

"Sean's just a person like you," she says. "Not everyone can be perfect like Alex."

"What does that mean?"

"Just forget it, I'm sorry. Like you said, let's not fight."

"You don't understand how serious this is," I reply, unwilling to back down.

"He's just hurting, and it's because of me," she says. I nod, it's always all about Kylee.

"That talk about my dad's Camaro—it would kill him, you know that?" I say.

"For God's sake, Bret, you're not onstage. Don't be so melo-dramatic!"

"You don't know what that car means to him." I concentrate on the taillight in front of me, trying to block out the image of my father standing in his grease-covered overalls, a Marlboro in his mouth, and hatred in his eyes as they take away from him the thing that matters most. It would be like taking away both his dreams of a better future and a memento of the only happy time in his hard life. "You don't know the first thing about my father."

"What are you saying?" Her voice is tense and tired.

"Nothing," I reply, unsure of what I am saying, feeling, or be-lieving.

"Just hire a lawyer, I don't see how—"

"How? With what money?" I respond. "I don't think one of your mother's ACLU friends is going to defend me for nothing, and besides, we all know that I did a number on Sean's SUV, and if that son of a bitch ever comes near you again, I'll go back for an encore!"

"Then just give him the money," Kylee says, sounding bored.

"With what? From where?" I bite my bottom lip again. "I quit my ushering job to spend more time with you. I'm sorry that I don't have unlimited resources like Sean."

"Can't you stop whining!"

"What does that mean?" I ask the question, knowing full well the answer. She turns away and pretends to sleep. Kylee can be so mean sometimes, even if she doesn't want to be. We drive home in silence, but then share "sorrys" along with good-night kisses.

"Cutie, as long as we love each other, none of this other stuff matters," she says, before going inside. A small bruise is probably forming under my shirt from Hitchings's hate tap; he might as well have punched me in the heart. I take the long way home, taking a driving tour of these days of turmoil, passing by Will's house, where the party still goes on, then past Sean's and a quick Hitchings house drive-by. I drive by Venus, spying the Crown Vic in the parking lot, and know Alex is there with Elizabeth. She's no doubt consoling him about the evening, rather than confronting and confounding him like Kylee did with me. Next, I drive over to the Rock, which has been painted over many times since last fall. I think about all the hurts and humiliations I've been trying to paint over, like knowing that Kylee and Bret, like Radio-Free Flint, won't be forever. Finally, I end the evening in front of the Grand Trunk tracks, looking at the words "Bret Lives" and wondering why anyone should even care.

Twenty-four
April 21–24, Junior Year

You did what?"

Dad pulls his head from under the hood of the Camaro, while I pull my head out of my ass and tell him about the hammer, the nails, and Sean's comeuppance. Now it's time for mine.

"His father said he would sue us and take everything, including the Camaro."

"Like hell!" my dad barks, wiping the grease from his hands.

I breathe a sigh of relief, as he lights up a smoke. "What are we going to do?"

"He's not getting this car!" Dad shouts, but I'm sensing his anger isn't directed at me.

"Well, let's fight it then," I offer. "We'll get our own lawyer."

"Lawyers!" Dad sneers, taking out his smoke so he can spit on the garage floor. "Do you know how much those bloodsuckers charge by the hour?"

"Bloodsuckers?" I repeat back, unsure if I'm asking for explanation or agreeing.

"You know the old saying, those who can't do, teach? Well, those who can't do or teach sue the rest of us who can. Bloodsucking scum!"

My father maybe just told a joke. It's not that funny, but I want to applaud the effort, so I fake it and force a chuckle.

"A good lawyer will want money up front, and we just don't have any saved," Dad says.

I swallow hard. I've been hoping there was a secret college fund set aside for me, but once again my father plays magician and with one sentence makes my hope vanish.

"Even if we had the money—which we don't—why bother? We'd only lose."

"What do you mean?"

"Did you do it?" He hands me enough rope to hang myself.

"Yes," I say calmly, all of his don't-lie-to-me lectures paying off.

"This is what I've been telling you, Bret, trying to teach you," he says, looking me right in the eye. "It's called consequences, accepting responsibility, being a man."

"What are we going to do?" I ask.

He pauses and grinds the butt into the floor. "I'll talk to this kid's father."

"And?" Dad's a big guy, but he's no Stone Cold or street fighter.

"I'm going to find out how much damage you did and then give him the money."

"How are you going to afford to do that?" I ask, having just learned that we are more or less broke.

My father nods, and then points toward the house. "There's a newspaper on the table. I suggest you look in the want ads for a real job, so we can work out a payment plan."

"But I don't have time to work." I sigh as my subtle protest.

My father laughs, not because I've said something smart and hilarious. "There's always time to work. Make it."

"But—"

"Don't do the crime, if you can't do the time."

"But Sean seemed serious about suing us," I remind my father.

"I'll talk to his dad, and we'll work something out."

"I'm sorry I did it, but I don't see how—"

"He only knows the card we've got showing. In seven card, you get four cards up, and three down," he explains. "The other people at the table don't know what cards you got down."

"And what do we have down?" I'm struggling with a vocabulary as mysterious as that of manifolds, carburetors, and pistons.

"A whole lot of nothing," he admits.

I'm lost. "So, how do—"

"His dad doesn't know that. Bret, it may surprise you to know your old man is actually good at something. I'm a pretty good poker player. I can bluff with the best of 'em. I can't tell you how many times I had squat and bluffed my way into winning the pot. Contrary to what your mom thinks, poker isn't just about smoking, swearing, and shooting the bull."

"But isn't bluffing just another word for lying?" I say, playfully riffing on my dad's rock-solid ethics.

"Not really. It's more a matter of not telling the whole truth."

"But what if he wants the money now?"

"I'll arrange the terms, you'll work it off," he says, pointing at the house. "You better get."

"But I promised Kylee I'd spend more time with her."

Dad shakes his head. "How old are you?"

He knows my age, probably by the number of days, but I tell him, anyway. "Almost seventeen."

His hard face goes soft. "There'll be other girls."

"But I love her. I want Kylee, I want—"

My dad interrupts me. "Again I ask: who told you that you could have what you want?"

I don't say anything. My father motions for us to sit down at his workbench.

"Bret, do you think I want to work in a car wash? Do you think this is the life I wanted when I was your age? I just wanted to own a cool car, hang with my friends, and party."

"And you did those things," I say, figuring two out of three still ain't bad.

"And a lot more I didn't count on," he says. My dad looks tired.

"What's that?" I ask. I'm beyond curious at my father's simple life that suddenly now seems very complicated.

"I told you already," he says softly. "Responsibility, discipline. It's called being a man."

"Still—"

"Bret, listen, when you're seventeen, you think mostly about yourself, and that's fine. But that's not life at forty, or even at thirty. Hell, it wasn't for me at twenty."

"I know," I say, trying to be an empathy machine like Mom.

"No, you don't. You don't know anything until you've lived it, every single day. It's not about getting what you want, it's about getting what you need and doing what you should."

I pause, take a deep breath, and ask the question, in part hoping that he'll ask me the same question one day, and that I'll have a decent answer. "Come on, Dad, what do you want?"

"A drink," he says without hesitation. I can see this is hard for him, but it's the only way he knows. "Your mom doesn't like that I let you smoke, and it may kill you in the end, but it won't destroy your life along the way. I remember when your mother went to the hospital in labor with you, and she gave me a choice. She told me she wouldn't be bringing you home if there was a single bottle in the house. So, while you came into this world, I said good-bye to drinking forever. I think it was a pretty good trade-off, even if it's a struggle every damn day."

He gets off the stool and walks a few steps to grab his wallet. He pulls out a few bills, and hands them to me. "Here's an advance on your first paycheck to starting paying Sean. And here's another advance so you can buy yourself some normal clothes and can get a real job."

Even though I'm still seated, I realize we've just taken one step back for the two we went forward as I pat my brand-new bright white Speed Racer T-shirt. "Not like this?"

"Why the hell do you dress like that? Where do you think it's going to get you?"

"It's cool. Besides, it's different from everybody else."

"Hard way," Dad says, shaking his head again.

"Like father, like son?" I try to make the tone light.

He shakes his head, trying to purge the grin forming on his weathered face. "Maybe."

I bound from the stool and stand next to the Camaro. "I feel sorry for Sean's dad."

"Why's that?"

"He doesn't know the cards you're holding," I say, realizing I didn't either, until now.

"Well, life's dealt him some pretty good cards," he says, pushing the analogy rather than pushing me away.

I let out a loud laugh, then shout. "He ain't shit. I think it's time."

"For what?" Dad asks.

I hand him his cell phone. "Like they say in poker: call!"

My dad actually laughs at something I've said. Another step forward.

When I told Kylee about needing to get a job, it led to another in an endless string of arguments in our month back together. We're fighting more, and not just for the make-up sex. The news I'd be working more and seeing her less led to what wrestling announcers call a slobberknocker. She threw me out of her house before I could even throw on all of my clothes. She was yelling and crying, while I fled the house, leaving behind my new Speed Racer T-shirt and my old green Chucks. I stood outside her house half naked and full-blown angry at her, my dad, and Sean. We went the whole weekend without speaking. I spent the time looking for work, hating myself, and dreading my first Monday-morning money meeting with Sean.

"There he is," Alex says, the words distorted through an early-Monday-morning yawn.

I look up from my book, *Sit-Down* by Sidney Fine, and see Sean's smirking face in the window of the library door, with Hitchings by his side.

"This is so humiliating," I tell Alex, looking at the floor.

"Have you seen his SUV lately?" Alex asks.

"No," I reply, proud of my discipline.

"He's got one of those 'Whoever Has the Most Toys Wins' bumper stickers," Alex says.

I motion for Sean to come into the library and over to our table. I want to get this over with. I look at my book to avoid eye contact. I want to see as little of him as possible.

"Where's my cash?" Sean asks, hard to understand as he and

Hitchings cackle. I don't look up. I just reach into my pocket and hand over the money Dad gave me until I land a job.

"Here you go," I say, staring down at his feet, which sport a pair of beaten-up green high-top Chuck Taylor All Stars.

I squint up into the blinding light of a new lie. Sean stands with Hitchings attached at the hip, plunging his knife in my back, and although she isn't there, Kylee's helping him twist it in.

"Bret, isn't that your—" Alex starts, but they cut him off with a shared roar of laughter.

"Shirt." The word spits out of my mouth like a broken tooth when I realize that Sean's wearing not just my shoes, but also my new Speed Racer T-shirt, last seen in Kylee's bedroom.

Twenty-five

Bret, what do you want to do?"

Mr. Douglas motions for me to sit down in his small office, my emotions out of control.

"It's about *Harvey*," I say, referring to the spring school play. I've missed a week of school and rehearsals.

"Well?" He's going to make me say the words, but it's hard. The leading role is perfect for me: a guy who sees something no one else sees.

"I have to drop out of *Harvey*," I say quickly, hoping that like removing a Band-Aid, the sudden pain will be preferable to a slow tear. "And not just the lead, but the whole show."

"I see." He nods. He seems to realize that I'm onto his moves, just as I'm sure he knows mine. "Have you really thought about this?"

"I just can't do it, Mr. Douglas. I'm sorry for letting you down again, but I can't concentrate on the play," I say, my acting skills allowing me to hold back tears.

"I'm sorry to hear that," he says. "How about being on the crew or stage manager?"

"No, I just can't," I say with all the strength I can muster.

"Bret, do you want to talk about what's really going on?"

What I want to say is, "I don't want to talk to anyone if they can't take away this hurt, anger, and madness, and if they can't do that, then screw 'em!" It's hard to talk about with anyone, even Dad and Alex. They both knew getting back with Kylee was wrong, and they both told me. I didn't listen, since I couldn't hear with my heart. I have so much to say, I stay silent.

"Okay. If you change your mind, the door's always open," Mr. Douglas says. "I mean that, I can't figure out how to lock the thing."

He pauses, waiting for the laugh that doesn't come.

"Bret, you have to stay connected to something. To the theater, your music, something."

"Why bother?" I'm not just defeated; I'm deflated and totally destroyed.

"Don't talk like that, Bret," he says with force. "Look at that stage over there. The roles I gave you up there were too small for your talent. Never deny that talent. Never deny yourself."

"But when I am myself, I just get beaten up and I can't fight back," I confess.

"Everybody fights back," he says.

"People like Dr. King never fought back," I say, recalling what the posters from the Edmonds's house taught me. I wonder how MLK would have handled a dream stealer like Sean.

"Yes, he did. He fought back using words and ideas, just not with violence," he says.

"And he got assassinated for it," I say, thinking how Kylee knocked me off.

"Bret, listen to what I'm saying," Mr. Douglas says, his voice impassioned. "If you want to deal with the Bob Hitchings of the world, you can't let them push you around."

"Then what should I do?" I ask him.

"I don't know. You'll need to decide that for yourself," Mr. Douglas says. "But I know just about the worst thing that you can do is to continue to do nothing."

"Like Principal Morgan?"

"Mr. Morgan's my boss. We disagree from time to time, but I don't think he's evil. And I don't believe anyone's all bad. I'm a big believer in gray areas."

"What does that mean?" I ask with a shrug.

"Remember at the start of the year when everybody got a student handbook?"

I shrug. I'm totally lost, but always willing to loyally follow Mr. Douglas.

"Did you read it?"

"No, I thought I'd wait for the movie," I say, still in touch with my sarcastic side.

"Well, we're talking to Brad Pitt's people about playing me, but that's beside the point," Mr. Douglas jokes, but I still can't manage a laugh. "The book spells out what you can and can't do at Southwestern. We have rules, and people have to follow them so things go smoothly."

I serve up another shrug, this time without a side of snide.

"It's a twenty-page book, so not every single situation is covered, right?"

If I shrug again, he's going to think I'm having an epileptic seizure. "I guess not."

"There's right, wrong, and then there's everything else. That's the gray area. It's where everyone makes choices, and it's my job—and Mr. Morgan's—to help students make the best ones. The best choices don't benefit just the individual. We're trying to have a society here."

"You should teach social studies." I get up to leave, and Mr. Douglas stands up as well.

"I have one more question to ask you," he says, shaking my hand, man to man.

"What's that?"

He gives me a light pat on the back, then delivers his line with an arched eyebrow and the comic timing that I can only hope one day to achieve. "Do you really think Brad Pitt is right for the part?"

Twenty-six

Bret, what are you thinking?"

It's Becca Levy. I expected and accepted this. "Look, let me explain—"

"I did you a favor and you stab me in the back?" she says, eyes wide with shock.

"No, listen, it's not like that!" I put my name in to run against her for Student Council President, selling out just like Alex predicted. I needed to do what Kylee's parents and Mr. Douglas and even Dad had told me: stand up for myself. I also need something to focus on 100 percent, aside from Kylee. That was Sean's job now. When I saw him in my shoes and shirt, I knew Kylee was a case-closed issue. I couldn't deal with the hurt, so I redirected it as best I could by righting another wrong. Morgan lied to me last fall. I never got my speech published. This is my chance to dust it off and shove my words up his ass in public. Kylee killed me, so there's nothing Morgan can do to destroy a dead man walking.

"I'm very upset," Becca says, then touches my shoulder. We're standing by my locker, which is emptier now that I've cleared out any evidence of Kylee. My vision is clear now that it's no longer clouded by her. One betrayal you can forgive, even it you can't forget, but two are unforgivable and unforgettable.

"I don't think I'll win. In fact, Becca, let me be honest with you," I say, trying to add some truth back into my life. "I don't even want to win. If I win, I'll quit and give it you. So you win, either way. This is really a favor for you."

"Why are you running if you don't want to win?"

"Because I want to make my speech," I say, keeping my voice down.

"About what?" Becca asks, ugly tears fading, her pretty smile emerging.

"About what happens at this school," I explain. "About how there's money for a sports team, but not for a speech team. How people like Hitchings get a free ride, and coaches like King get away with being lousy teachers. I'm tired of this hypocrisy and my apathy about it."

"Why in God's name would you want to do that?" Becca asks.

"Because it's the most fun I can have without being expelled," I say glibly. This isn't about winning, and in the end it isn't about Kylee's betrayal; it's about finally fighting back. I wasn't going to do it wrong again. I'd use my best tools and talents. I loved being onstage, but I was tired of acting the part of victim. I'm tired of everything and everyone pounding on me. I'm hurting worse than any person could hurt, I'm going to exploit it. I'm no nail, so screw them all.

"Bret, that sounds like a bad idea," Becca says.

"That's why it sounds so right," I say, trying to make her laugh. "I need to take a stand."

"You won't need a stand, you'll need a shield," Becca jokes, and I laugh.

"I guess what I really need is courage."

"It's like the *Wizard of Oz*. You need courage and people like Bob need brains."

"So which one of us needs a heart?" I ask, knowing that mine is too broken to function.

"Both you and Bob have plenty of heart. That's the real problem I think."

"Maybe, except for one small thing."

"What's that?" she asks.

"They hate me and Alex, and anyone who's not like them," I say. Then, for effect, I raise my voice to deliver an old pro-wrestling catchphrase: "I don't hate the players, I hate the game."

"If that's your campaign slogan, then I don't have anything to worry about, because I'm sure you won't win."

"Bring it on!" I shout. "The way I see it, you did me a favor getting the reformed Radio-Free Flint to play at the prom, so if I do win, I'll be doing a favor for you in return."

"Could you do me one more little favor then?" she says, her smile growing brighter.

"What's that?" I ask.

"Since I got you to the prom, could you get me there?" she says with just the right amount of bashfulness. "I don't have a date, and I thought maybe we could—"

"Becca, why would you want to be seen with me?" I ask to cover what would otherwise be my stunned silence, also wondering why she doesn't have a date with Will. She's smart, involved, and is way more popular than me. She's no ten, but then again, neither am I. I learned that math lesson hard.

"Because you're more than just a mental babe," she says, speaking into the floor.

I pause again, the clashing of emotion ringing in my brain,

heart, and every cell in between. "Okay, but you've got to promise me one thing," I say.

"What's that?" she says, with a prettier smile than I ever noticed.

"You won't talk to the drummer!" I shout melodramatically.

"Cross my heart, Bret," she says, asking no follow-up question, which confirms what I suspected. I'm guessing that Sean told Hitchings who probably told everybody he could about Sean walking in my shoes. "Are you sure about this?"

"One hundred percent!" I will show everybody while you can knock me down, I'll get back up every time. When you've got nothing to lose, there's nothing to do but win. "Deal?"

"Deal," she says, shaking my hand, holding it longer than I expected. "Besides, what's the worst that could happen?"

Twenty-seven

We'll hear first from Becca Levy, then from Bret Hendricks."

Becca gets up as Mr. Popham, the student council sponsor, sits down. As Becca walks past me, I sense that she doesn't seem the least bit self-conscious about people not liking what she says, who she is, or how she looks. She is pretty, but things onstage are about to get very ugly very quickly when I step up to the microphone. This is the final speech: we've done grades nine and ten, now my people, the juniors, get their chance to listen. In my speeches to those young ones, I was pulling punches. But this last one, with Hitchings, Bison, and Sean in attendance, is going to be what wrestler's call a shoot: the truth and nothing but the truth.

I see Sean and do a half smirk, half smile. I'm still angry at him from when I handed over his money in the library, but it doesn't stick. I can forgive him more easily than Kylee because I know what it is like to fall in love with her, to lose her, and be betrayed by her. We'll always have that in common. I hope that along with learning the history of the United States, Sean's also studying the history of the Destroyed Mates of Kylee Edmonds.

When I met her, she cheated on Chad with me. The question for Sean isn't who, but when. There's no sense in even asking why.

"Bret Hendricks," Mr. Popham says after Becca finishes, inviting me up to the microphone. After the applause for her dies down, I bring myself back to life.

"Flint Southwestern High School is run by a cult: the cult of jockarchy. It's like any other cult. They wear their cult colors, worship at the altar of athletic achievement, and scorn those who do not believe as they do. A conformity cult of the privileged."

I look over at Mr. Popham, who is frowning and now standing next to Mr. Douglas in the wings. I haven't seen Morgan yet, but I expect I will. Mold King Cold isn't in attendance; he probably has sports scores to read or plays to diagram.

"You walk in the door, and it hits you like a bloody nose: a red sea of Spartan jackets. It's like walking in on a cult meeting. They have their secret symbols, their letter system, and their charismatic coaches who act as their leaders." I'm calm, yet concerned, as I see the teachers in the audience getting uncomfortable. Some of the students are getting off on what I'm saying, while Hitchings, Bison, and the bullyboys look ready to attack. Sean just looks amused.

"They want everyone to believe as they do, and those of us who don't are pushed out. They are the only majority cult, and I'm sick of them. Sick of the ball-throwing, puck-passing, track-running thick skulls." I'm slightly sidetracked by the sight of one of the teachers exiting out the back, sprinting toward the office.

"Let me make myself clear, I don't mean everyone who picks up a ball belongs to this cult," I say, winking at Will Kennedy. "In a larger sense, it's not really about sports but about trying to have a great society rather this tyranny of the strong over the weak. I reject a world where some people push and take, while the rest of us try to pull together and give back."

The room is getting loud, which bothers me not, since I'm shouting my long held words.

"Sports has to be about winners and losers, we all understand that, but that doesn't mean we have to live that way off the playing field. Let's stop bullying each other. Let's stop acting big by putting others down," I say, happy I've worked some of my mom's philosophy into my speech, even though when she read it, she urged me not to give it, for fear I'd get in trouble. She's right, trying to protect me as usual, but the real trouble is all around, and I refuse to ignore it any longer.

"Why should you vote for me? Simple: because I think many of you are as tired of what happens here at school as I am. I think a lot of you are fed up with a jockarchy who thinks the world revolves around them and harass those who are different."

I look into the audience to see Hitchings's face has turned as red as his letter jacket.

"Earlier this year, we did a play on this stage called *The Crucible* by Arthur Miller," I tell the crowd, since probably no more than a handful in the audience attended the show. "The play's about the Salem witch trials, but it's really a metaphor about the 1950s and the McCarthy era, where everybody was supposed to conform. No one called this McCarthy guy on his bully tactics until a TV reporter named Edward R. Murrow took him on, but not by making a speech like this. Instead, Murrow let McCarthy destroy himself with his own vile and repulsive words."

I reach into my pocket, and I think I heard a few people gasp in fear, but I pull out nothing more than paper filled with words, the most powerful weapon of all.

"I went to the library this morning and, with Mrs. Sullivan's help, I found this article from *Time* magazine a few weeks after Columbine. This article quotes a member of that school's jockarchy, but it sounds so similar to what I've heard here at our school." I now look at my audience, asking them to agree to my vision by showing them the viciousness of the alternative.

"'Columbine is a clean, good place except for those rejects. Sure we teased them. But what do you expect with kids who come to school with weird hairdos and horns on their hats? It's not just jocks; the whole school's disgusted with them. They're a bunch of homos. If you want to get rid of someone, usually you tease 'em. So the whole school would call them homos.'" I put the paper back in my pocket, then wipe the sweat from my brow.

Then, just as Morgan appears, and is about to shut off the microphone, I hit the finish.

"The enemy's in this room, but we are not afraid to be ourselves. We are not afraid and we will not be victims any longer!" I shout, pointing right at Hitchings. I thrust my arms in the air, middle fingers curled inward, but in my heart aimed at the scarlet sea of water walkers. As I leave the stage, Morgan follows me, the veins in his neck bulging like ivy along his neck. I have no intention of dodging this bullet. This is about accepting responsibility.

Instead of yelling, he speaks firmly and almost with a smile. "I warned you before about mentioning Columbine. You almost caused a riot in there, and you know what that means?"

I don't give him the satisfaction of even making eye contact.

"You're suspended, Bret Hendricks, and pursuant to school policy, you're expelled from school," he declares.

"Why?" I know why, but I ask anyway; it's tough to break old bad habits.

He slowly holds up one finger at a time, mouthing the words "One, two, three."

I smile back at him and reply by holding up one finger. The middle one.

Twenty-eight

o the crime . . ."

". . . do the time," I say, finishing my father's sentence as we finish off dinner. While my father's loosened up on me somewhat, when it comes to issues of right and wrong, law and order, he remains rigid.

"Can I be excused?" Robin asks in her unvarying whine. For someone who used to be such a cute kid, she's become a real middle school snot. Just like I was. However, unlike me, she'll probably graduate from her school this year.

I tell my parents about the events of yesterday and the meeting tomorrow. I still can't tell Dad that this suspension is my exit pass. He knows about this episode but not previous incidents.

"I told you this would happen," Mom says; she's quite upset.

"I'm going to call Mrs. Edmonds and ask for her help," I say softly, almost ashamed.

"Do whatever you have to do, Bret," she says curtly, getting up from the table.

"What's that busybody going to do?" Dad asks.

"She told me she knew a lawyer who might help me."

"Bret, I can't afford a lawyer, and even if I could . . ." he says, looking away from me.

"Bloodsuckers."

"It's not that. What the hell were you thinking, trying to cause a riot?"

"That I was tired of not fighting back."

"Still," my father mutters in a tone of voice that tells me he can see my point.

"Don't worry about the money," I reassure him. "He's pro bono from the ACLU."

"No good liberal do-gooders!" Dad says, but he's smiling about it.

"I'm going to call," I say, getting up from the table. I decide to take a pass through the kitchen, where Mom's washing the dishes. "Mom?"

"I'm busy, Bret," she says, keeping focused on the task at hand.

"Look, I'm sorry. It's not that I like Mrs. Edmonds better than you."

"Don't be silly," she says dismissively, her body language telling a different story. The soapy water ripples as her hands are submerged and shaking.

"You were there for me before, and you stood up for me. Thank you."

"You're my son."

"But I know there's only so much even you can do," I say, trying to reassure her. "I know if you could help me more, you would. It's just that Mrs. Edmonds has—"

"It's okay, Bret, really," she says, the steam rising from the sink as her jealousy subsides.

"Thanks, Mom." I give her a big and long-overdue hug.

The next morning, Mrs. Edmonds and the ACLU lawyer, Mr. Cunningham, meet me at school. On the phone the night before, we'd gone over my campaign creed and the stuff that had happened at school that led up to the speech. Mr. Cunningham was cool, but he said that the ACLU would only do the free-speech stuff gratis; I would have to call his office if I wanted to pursue any sort of legal action. I told him no, and not just because of the cost, but because court wasn't the place to settle the issues between Hitchings and me. That day's coming soon, especially after my speech, which I sense has moved up our destiny date. This was a battle I would have to fight alone, with support but no backup.

"You ready, son?" Mom asks. She also came with me this morning to meet with the lawyer. While I talk with him, she and Mrs. Edmonds go into the other room for coffee. They have nothing in common, except for being mothers and caring about me. Two hard cases.

"Don't worry, Bret," Mrs. Edmonds tells me. "We're behind you one hundred percent."

I nod. Just because her daughter hurt me doesn't mean she won't help me. Mr. Edmonds quoted Tom Joad's speech from *The Grapes of Wrath* ("Whenever a guy is kicking another guy, I'm there") to explain why they felt so strongly about issues involving underdogs, like me.

"And who's this?" Principal Morgan inquires as we enter the conference room. Mr. Douglas is there, and so is Mrs. Pfeil. There's also a guy in a suit I don't know.

"Mike Cunningham, Michigan Civil Liberties Union," my lawyer says, handing Mr. Morgan his card and shaking the hand of the mystery man standing next to Morgan.

"Curtis Walker. I'm the school board lawyer," he says, returning the handshake. We all sit down at the table. "We're here to talk about Bret's suspension and—"

"About our pending suit regarding Bret's free-speech rights," Mr. Cunningham interjects.

"What?" Morgan says, apoplectic. It's the last thing he says, as the lawyers go at it for almost an hour. My head gets dizzy listening to it all. Dad's wrong: lawyers aren't bloodsuckers; they don't stop talking long enough to suck anyone's blood. Mr. Cunningham talks about something called *Tinker versus Des Moines*, which sounds like a wrestling match, while Walker counters with *Island Trees* and verbal-assault statutes.

All the while, Morgan sits there getting madder, while my never-to-be-mother-in-law Mrs. Edmonds looks calm and collected. Mrs. Pfeil and Mr. Douglas just sit on the school's side of the table, even though I know they're really on mine.

Finally, Mr. Walker and Mr. Morgan start whispering to each other. Mr. Cunningham doesn't say anything; he gives a big thumbs-up. I keep my hands in my pockets for safety's sake.

"Mrs. Hendricks, here is what we propose," Walker finally says. "As the speech took place on school grounds, Bret is subject to the rules of this school, contrary to what Mr. Cunningham might have you believe. With apologies to Justice Fortas and the *Tinker* decision, the Constitution sometimes does stop at the schoolroom door."

I wait for Cunningham to reply, but he's silent and smiling like a friendly shark.

"However, while your son's speech was certainly offensive to many at the school, it did not constitute a verbal threat, urge others toward violence, endanger other students, or—"

Cunningham interrupts: "You had a right to say what you did," he says, looking at me.

"If that's the case, then I'm not suspended, right?" I ask, this time not sure of the answer.

"Not so fast, smart guy!" Morgan says, glaring at me. "You forgot your message to me."

"What's he talking about?" Mr. Cunningham asks. I'd not mentioned my exit gesture.

"I flipped Mr. Morgan off when—"

"That changes everything." Walker says imperiously. "That's conduct, Bret, not speech. You don't have the right to show that type of disrespect to teachers or staff." Walker is now riding high in the driver's seat.

Morgan's all smiles. "So for that reason, you'll be suspended, which means—"

"Why and when did you do this?" Mom asks, her voice shaking along with her hands.

"After he told me . . ." I started, then just slumped, defeated, in my chair.

"After I told him he was expelled," Morgan answers for me.

"Wait just a second," Mr. Douglas says, finally entering the fray.

"What is it?" Morgan snarls, shooting him a look that doesn't encourage free speech.

"Well, if he thought he was expelled—" Mr. Douglas says, looking at Mom.

"Then he didn't think he was in school," Mom says. "I don't see how you can punish him for something he did once you told him he was expelled." I don't know if that's true, but Morgan's frowning, which is a very good sign.

"That's a minor point, a technicality," Morgan says while Walker sighs.

"The law is about minor points and technicalities," Mr.

Cunningham says, weighing in. "If you proceed with his suspension, the ACLU will get involved in a major way."

Mrs. Edmonds, who has been sitting back away from the table, finally speaks. "And I'll see to it that the voters of Flint get involved. You have a school-bond referendum next year, I believe."

"Who are you again?" Morgan asks, unaccustomed to being on the other end of a threat.

"My name is Margaret Edmonds. I'm on the board of the North End Food Bank, and I also serve on the board of several Flint organizations," Mrs. Edmonds says softly, but strongly. Clearly, she is now in charge. "I'm here to support my good friend Bret Hendricks."

"Mrs. Edmonds, this is very complicated and your involvement—" Morgan starts to say.

Mrs. Edmonds walks up to the table and puts one hand on my shoulder while the other clutches her cell phone. "Mr. Morgan, don't try to patronize me. Nor will you try to silence me from speaking as you did Mr. Hendricks. I know everyone in this town, including the mayor and your friend Hank, whom I know very well from my work in the community."

As Mrs. Edmonds tears Morgan a new one, I ask Mr. Cunningham, "Who's Hank?"

"Henry T. Collins, the school superintendent. Morgan's boss," he replies calmly.

"If you want your bond passed, then think very seriously about how you handle this situation," Mrs. Edmonds says in an icy tone. "You don't want to get on my bad side."

"Now, let's not get too excited about this. We can work something out." Morgan is backpedaling so fast I'm surprised he doesn't fall ass-backward.

"We can work it out here and now or on the *Flint Journal*'s front page and on the six o'clock news. I will tell them to cover me, my allies, and the ACLU practicing our right to free speech and assembly at every school board meeting and every public event."

With those words, Mrs. Edmonds has turned the conference room into her kitchen, and the heat is more than Morgan can stand. Walker taps Morgan on the shoulder, and they have a ten-minute-long whispering conference on their side of the table. Our side is perfectly still.

"Mr. Morgan believes strongly . . ." Mr. Walker finally says but is distracted when Mrs. Edmonds starts dialing. "Mrs. Edmonds, let me finish! He believes strongly that Mr. Hendricks should be expelled. However, I have persuaded him that it's in no one's best interest to argue the fine points of this case in private or in public. Also, as it's the end of the school year, Mr. Morgan is willing to let this episode pass without further incident or argument, on one condition."

"What's that?" I ask, reminding everyone, since it's my life they're discussing, that I'm still alive.

Morgan won't look at me. "We counted the votes after school and you won. You got more votes than Becca Levy. I'll let this go, if you resign."

"The school district can't have a principal and a Student Council President with such personal animosity, and I'm sure you'll agree with me Mrs. Edmonds," Walker says.

"Regardless, the point—" Mrs. Edmonds responds.

"I'll take it," I say, bluffing with a poker face that would make Dad proud.

"Are you sure?" my mom asks, but I'm very firm. Like everyone else in the room, she's unaware that my original intention was to resign if I'd won.

"Positive," I say, holding back the Stone Cold catchphrase. The bottom line is that I'm not Austin, and post-Kylee, I'm not the same Bret Hendricks anymore.

As I look around the room, I'm grateful others have stood up for me. I realize that now I need to stand up for myself. In the past month, Sean has taken away the only girl I've ever loved, but every day for the past three years, Hitchings has taken away something even more important: my dignity. I can't get Kylee back; I'll get myself back instead.

Like I'd once prophesized in this very conference room, a day of reckoning is coming. But the revelation stuns me: it's not Hitchings's reckoning I've been dreaming about all of these years, but my own. *My own.*

"Let's go home," Mom says, words that hold a huge appeal for me. Leaving the conference room, I vow never to set foot in there again. I'm as tired of my own petty acts of rebellion as I am of Morgan's military rule. If I could survive Kylee, I can survive anything.

After some small talk, we start to leave. Before we do, I give Mrs. Edmonds a big hug. "Wow, that was something!" I almost shout. "But how did you know Morgan would give in?"

"He's just a bully in a bad blue suit," Mrs. Edmonds says as we share in the satisfaction that barking underdogs can still sometimes come out on top.

Twenty-nine

Great show!"

"Really?" I ask. Like Kylee, I need reinforcement of facts I already know.

"Really!" Becca says, then gives me a hug, even if my sweaty T-shirt will ruin her beautiful ivory prom dress, which looks great with her curled dark-black hair. She's not wearing ruby red slippers to stand out, but she looks outstanding. She was going to wear a violet dress, but I talked her out of it.

"Thank God that's over," Alex says of our gig, then waves at Elizabeth. She's far too funky in her red spiky hair, red tank top, and black leather pants for this room full of uptight tuxes and too-tight little blue dresses. Our new full-time drummer, Will, who took my side at school in the post-debate lunchroom discussions, heads back to his date, some cheerleader type that Alex can't abide. The DJ wastes no time in killing our buzz by booming out bad R & B.

"You want to dance?" Becca asks as the slow song slithers from the DJ's speakers.

"Love to, but first Alex and I are gonna have a smoke. Come with?" I respond.

"No thank you!" she says, her disapproval unbending and ongoing.

"I've got to wind down after the show," I say in my defense. I've stopped smoking, for the most part, because of Becca. I'm trying to do a better job of listening than I did with Kylee.

"Okay, but hurry back," she says, squeezing my hand. Becca turns to talk to Elizabeth, and its like summer theater all over viewing this odd couple.

I give Becca a quick kiss on the cheek, while Alex just winks Elizabeth's way, then we make our exit. Despite the sweat running down my face, I put my tux jacket back on. I feel nothing but the cool of the evening running through my hair as Alex and I step out the back door of the Flint Country Club.

"Freak faggots." The welcoming comment comes from Hitchings.

"Let's go," Alex says, and turns around to leave like so many times before.

"No, I'm done with this bullshit," I say firmly to Alex, even if I want to shout it out to the smokers, tokers, and drinkers gathered on the dimly lit loading dock. When I don't say anything to Hitchings, he turns his attention back to his buddies and the bottle they're sharing.

"Are you sure?" Alex asks. I nod, and we light up our Camels.

"I'm not worried about him," I say, feeling strangely calm. "Besides, he's all punched out."

"What do you mean?"

"Will asked me to come watch him play baseball last week," I tell Alex, earning a smoke-filled sigh. He's warming up to Will's drumming skills, but not his normal-guy persona.

"So?"

"Will was pitching and Hitchings was catching," I say, indifferent to Alex's total disinterest in anything sports related. "In the fifth inning, there was a close play at home plate. The runner from Flint Central tried to score by running through Hitchings, but Hitchings demolished the guy. He didn't just block the plate and knock the runner on his ass. He tagged him so hard he broke the guy's nose, but he also dropped the ball, allowing the run to score."

"He's an asshole all the time, isn't he?" Alex asks.

I laugh loudly, gathering a few stares. "Anyway, in the next inning, Hitchings is batting, and the pitcher from Central throws the ball at him. Hitchings rushed the mound and threw this savage body block, knocking the guy down, and then he started punching out his lights."

"Sounds like your wrestling show, doesn't it?" Alex cracks, but I'm not laughing.

"The image I'll most remember is King wrapping his arms around Hitchings to keep him from throwing more punches. Hitchings's knuckles were smeared with blood and grass stains, and his face was contorted in a fanatical smile," I finish the story, noticing that Hitchings is a few feet away. He's flashing that same smile at Alex and me.

"You surprise me, Hendricks," Hitchings says, turning his attention away from the bottle and toward us. "I thought you'd be the one wearing a dress tonight and Alexandra the tux."

"Whatever, Bob. Whatever you want to say," I reply with my customary shrug. I look around and the dock seems to be filled with mostly unfriendly faces.

Hitchings laughs loudly and gulps his whiskey hard. "No speech, big mouth?"

"We're leaving," Alex says, taking a step toward the door, which opens to reveal two more unfriendly faces heading toward us: Sean and Kylee, aglow in love and clove smoke.

"Freak faggot, no wonder Kylee dropped your ass." Hitchings won't let it go.

I toss my smoke on the ground, then turn to face him. "That's an excellent use of alliteration for someone who's illiterate." It's a cheap shot and not true. Hitchings isn't an idiot; he just acts like one.

"What're you gonna do about it, faggot?" Hitchings says, raising both his voice and his fists.

Sticks and stones, and pencils, punches, and pushes—I had let it all go, and he had always won, but I realize that doesn't make me a loser at all. Regardless, I say, "Nothing at all."

"You two deserve each other," he says, coming right up against Alex, then poking him in the chest. Alex flinches and takes a step back while my anger builds. Hitchings is slurring his words, drowning in the Jack swimming in his skull. "You two faggots are fucking gutless."

"Gutless?" I repeat. As if by instinct, I look over at Kylee, and remember her describing me that way in her journal, one of the many paper cuts I suffered from reading it. "A gutless person would have run away, but I came back to school every day. A gutless person would be like all of you, picking on anyone a little bit different. How much guts does that take? You can call me a faggot or a freak, but don't you dare call me gutless. Just because I don't want to fight you doesn't make me gutless," I shout, feeling like a stone is thrown from around my neck.

"Big talk, no action. Like I said, gutless," Hitchings says, then laughs in Alex's face.

"You're just not worth the effort!" Alex yells. "You fugly sub-human—"

Before Alex completes his suicide note, Hitchings pushes him down to the ground and spits right in his face. "Freaks! I hate all you freaks!"

"I've had it with you, Hitchings!" I shout back at him as I remove my tux jacket.

"Cool it, Bret, he's not worth it," Alex says as he picks himself off the concrete.

"No, he's not," I say tossing my jacket at Hitchings. "But I am. And so are you."

Dad always asks me what I am going to do with myself, and I finally have an answer as I take two steps toward Hitchings, refusing to take one step back. He pushes me hard, but I keep my balance, then take a wild swing at him. But unlike during my scuffle with Sean, luck isn't smiling as my fist misses. Hitchings throws a body block on me, knocking me on my ass.

"Get up!" Hitchings growls.

"Stay down!" Alex yells, but all of my common sense has gone deaf.

"Fine, let's do this," I sing out, and feel as free and unafraid as I do onstage.

"Bret, no!" Kylee shouts, but the sound of her voice only steels my determination.

Hitchings laughs as I put my hands in front of me and shout. "Hitchings, I'm not afraid of you!"

"No!" Kylee screams again at me.

"Watch this," Hitchings sneers, leering at Kylee and pointing at Alex.

And they do.

He pushes me until I'm up against a wall. I push off and try to tackle him. My lame offensive attempt allows him to wrap his arms around my head, holding it in place near his waist.

"Blow me, faggot!" Hitchings shouts, slamming his right knee into my face. The first impact jolts me backward and twists my head. This isn't WWE, and Stone Cold isn't going to do a run-in to save my ass. My fantasy comes knee to face with my reality, as Hitchings slams his knee up again, exploding the blood vessels in my nose and mouth. "This will shut you up!"

Again and again.

I spit out a tooth, like a shooting star in the galaxy of blood and saliva dripping from my mouth. He throws one more knee, and I crumple onto the concrete.

"Had enough, you gutless pussy?" he yells out, then he spits on me as I roll away.

"I am . . . not . . . gutless," I say as best as I can through my recently rearranged mouth. From my kneeling position, I dive into his legs, but I can't move him. I see that some of the bullyboys are blocking the door, while Bison holds his arms out, keeping away anyone who might wish to stop the slaughter. Feeling safe and of unsound mind, Hitchings kicks me hard in the ribs.

Again and again.

The next time I spit, the blood's darker. I can barely move, and my body's in shock. Still, my brain won't shut down, nor will my broken mouth.

"That all you got . . . Hitchings?" I sputter, each word jabbing my lungs like razor blades. I don't have the energy to stand, so I hoist myself into a crawl. "Is that . . . all you got? You ain't shit!"

Hitchings answers with a hard punch to the top of my head. It's easy to hear, since it explodes directly into my skull. All around me, there's a wall of sound, and I realize this is like the WWE in one respect: we're giving people their money's worth. I hear a lone voice yelling for Hitchings to end his assault as his fist cracks my skull again and he finally cries out in pain. I know I've scored my first offensive move by breaking his right hand with my head.

"Bob, that's enough," a lone voice says, becoming more familiar.

I sense Hitchings standing over me. I crawl up on one elbow and swing my left fist into his knee. There's no sound, but he snaps back with another punch directly to my left ear, which sends me back to the concrete. As I lie on the ground, about all I can see are Hitchings's rented black shoes spattered with my blood, like paint.

"Bob, I said that's enough, okay?" the lone voice says, and I suddenly realize: it's Sean. Hitchings lands two stiff kicks into my ribs in answer to Sean.

"You're the gutless one," I say, but I don't think Hitchings hears me. I can barely move my mouth. I do, however, hear clearly the sound of Hitchings yelling in pain and shock as Sean knocks him down. With my eyes swelling shut, I can barely see Sean land six shots a second as he plays Hitchings face like a drum.

Finally, some teachers rush out, which is lucky for Hitchings; Sean's all over him. Morgan pulls Sean off, his blue suit and white shirt now candy-striped with blood.

"What a mess," Morgan says. "Let's get an ambulance in here."

"I already called 911," Kylee says, her voice filled with anxiety.

I roll over on my back. It's the only part of my body not in total agony. I can barely breathe from the stiff kicks to the ribs. The fight between Hitchings and Sean has broken up, as rent-a-guards hold them down. Sean's face is on the pavement, almost next to mine.

"Thanks, Sean," I gurgle out.

"I figured I owed you," Sean says, trying to catch his breath.

Hitchings is standing now, arms restrained, but not his mouth. "Hendricks, you—"

I gather what energy I have left, and cut him off: "You want more?"

"Shut up, Bret!" Morgan demands in a rough voice. "Just be quiet."

Kylee, with tears staining her violet dress, comes to check on me; I see her beautiful brown eyes looking down at me with kindness and guilt as I utter, "I'm not gutless."

"I know, Bret," she says, stroking my hair gently before she moves over toward Sean.

"Bret, what were you thinking?" Alex says, kneeling next to me with both Becca and Elizabeth at his side. Becca cradles my busted open head in her soft arms, not caring that my face is turning her ivory prom dress dark blood-red.

"I wasn't thinking," I say, trying to joke, but blood, not laughter, gurgles from my throat.

"But why did you try to fight him?" Alex asks.

"Don't ask why, Alex. Only ask what's next," I say, as the EMTs lean over me. Hitchings is gone; I hope taken to a waiting police cruiser. "Mr. Morgan, where are you?"

"What is it?" Morgan asks, kneeling down next to me.

"Tell Hitchings . . . ," I manage to say with my broken jaw and healed soul. "Tell him I'm not afraid of him anymore."

Thirty

Bret, are you awake?"

I don't respond to my father's query, not out of defiance, but because there's no real way to do so. My jaw is wired shut, and both of my eyelids are swollen over. My guts are damaged, but I finally showed that I have them.

"Bret, can you hear me?" Mom whispers.

I just lie there listening to hospital life go on around me. From what I've overheard, my injuries are extensive. I've got a bad concussion, a broken nose, a bruised eardrum, bruised ribs, a bruised kidney, five fewer teeth, and a jaw held together more by steel wire than human tissue.

"Mary, let him rest," I hear my father say softly. So softly it can't cover the sound of my mother's crying or of my father's uncharacteristic attempt to comfort rather than confront her.

"My baby boy," Mom says.

"This is my fault, my fault," I hear my father say, his voice growing fainter as his heavy footsteps lead away from the bed. "My fault, my goddamn stupid fault."

"Honey, please don't do this to yourself." Now it's Mom's turn to kick on her empathy machine, a device all hospitals should install. With only one good ear, I strain to hear them.

"I'm as bad a father as my dad," Dad says, pounding his foot or hand against the door.

"Don't say that," my mom says, but everybody in the room knows the truth.

"That Hitchings kid probably won't even go to jail for this, thanks to his dad," my father says. "His dad gets him out of jail, while Bret's old man puts him in a hospital bed. Damn it!"

Things go quiet for a long time, except for Mom's crying and Dad's trying not to.

"Mrs. Hendricks, can I come in?" I hear someone say from a distance.

"One second, Alex," my mother says. I hear both of my parents take a deep breath, composing themselves, trying to put the best face on things for my best friend.

"It's okay," my father mutters, even though he's no fan of Alex.

"How's he doing?" Alex says, the stress in his voice obvious to all.

"Bret has—" Mom starts, but tears stop her. "Excuse me, Alex."

"This is my fault," Alex says over the sound of a chair pulled closer to the bed.

"That doesn't help anybody," my dad says, sounding equally as nervous as Alex.

"He stood up for me," Alex says. "The thing with Kylee and Sean was also my fault."

"How so?" my father asks as he also pulls his chair closer to the bed.

I listened with pain exploding in every nerve cell still functioning as Alex spills his guts to Dad about everything that went down between Kylee, Sean, and me. He even told him about the stupid fight that Sean and I had over Christmas when Sean told me the way to get back at Hitchings was to let him beat me up and then sue him. He told Dad about Sean wearing my shirt to school. Alex told Dad how I stood up for him, leading to the prom carnage. All the while, I heard Dad's breathing get heavier and heavier, like a steam engine about to explode.

"Alex, why are you telling me this?" Dad finally asks.

"Because I thought you should know," Alex said. "Because if I had a dad, I would want him to know these things."

"That must have been hard for you, growing up without a father."

"Not really, Mr. Hendricks, not really," Alex says slow and sadly. "When your father dies, he rejects you once."

"I did my best for my boy," Dad says.

"He also did his best for you, and for me," Alex says softly. "That's the worst thing."

The door opens and I hear my mother's shoes on the tile floor again. "Alex, thanks for coming. We'll let you know when he can communicate."

"Sure thing," Alex says, then leans over me. Despite the swelling in my brain, my forehead accepts the kiss Alex plants above my eyes as he whispers: "Radio-Free Flint forever."

Once the door closes, I hear my parents talking, but they must have moved to the corner of the room because their words are hard to understand from this distance and one-ear deafness.

"I don't know, Mary, I don't know," my father says loudly after a while.

"We don't have any health insurance, so how are we going to pay for this?" Mom says.

"I said, I don't know!" My father is raging mad, not at me I guess, but at the world.

"Yes, you do," Mom says, but Dad's only reply is to slam the door behind him as he leaves the room. I imagine him sitting in his truck, smoking, and feeling as beat up as I do, except the only medicine he wants would kill him and his family in the long run. Down in the hospital parking lot, among the grieving families with lost loved ones and happy relatives of newborns, sits my father, trying to figure out the best decision to make when you don't have any good choices.

Thirty-one

Kylee's here to see you."

I sit up in my bed, which I'm now able to do without much pain. I sip water through a straw from the bottle next to me. Mom sticks her head in the door to repeat her announcement.

I hold up five fingers, signaling to her that I want five minutes to get myself together. Since getting out of the hospital I communicate with my parents mostly through Post-it notes and hand signals. But today is the first time I can actually talk again. Next time I see Mr. Douglas, I'll have to thank him for encouraging me to take that summer mime workshop before my sophomore year. You never know what lessons you need to learn sometimes until you need them. Maybe Austin is wrong: you can trust some people, like Mr. Douglas. He stopped by to invite me to work on the summer theater production. Becca visits all she can, but her schedule is pretty packed, working her first job and taking summer art classes. It's not the same as with Kylee, but that's okay. It's not worse or better, it's just different. I like different, but I think I've learned you can be a little different, like Becca, without feeling odd.

I'm hoping Becca won't be at odds with me after Kylee's visit today. She knows about it, and she's not happy, but like me, Becca's able to forgive. No wonder we're so compatible. Sean doesn't know or care, as he and Kylee have broken up, for reasons no doubt as explainable yet complex as the splitting of the atom or the breaking of the human heart.

Kylee's parents have dropped in often, usually with gifts, most recently a Bob Dylan CD set and a biography of Martin Luther King Jr. I still don't know how many roads a man must walk down, but standing up, being beat down, and then standing up again has to eat up some serious miles.

I wonder if Kylee will lose her lunch when she sees my new look. To do some of the medical work on me, the nurses had to modify my mane. I try to picture the glee in Dad's eyes as the techs shaved my head. Still, I don't think I'll let it grow back. I'll really look like a senior (citizen, that is) with my bald head. I'll look like Austin, and I'm feeling pretty stone-cold myself, but I think my days thinking any violence is entertaining are behind me.

Where my senior year is going to take place is still up in the air. Despite everything that's occurred, and all the hard lessons I've learned inside and outside of Southwestern, I don't want to leave my pals, Mr. Douglas, or Becca. There's a meeting on Monday, but I get the sense from Mom that in spite of Mrs. Edmonds's best efforts, my expulsion for fighting is serious and final. Also, I understand that getting beat up isn't considered a First Amendment issue.

I overheard my mom and dad talking at dinner, saying that Bob Hitchings's father is taking time out of his golf game to attend this meeting as well. I breathed a sigh of relief when Mr. Douglas told me that Hitchings is transferring to another school.

nailed

Supposedly, it's for more athletic challenges, but I think even Morgan and Mold King Cold know they've created a monster they need to cut loose. Hitchings knows his fate, and I'll know mine after this weekend.

Radio-Free Flint plans to cut a CD as soon as I can open my mouth to sing, not that we have any money to release it. Alex comes by nearly every day, playing demos. The first song on the CD will be one that he wrote just for me called "Faith in the Face of Adversity," although most of his songs still seem to be about Elizabeth.

I sit up in bed, then lean over to push away all the books collecting by the side of the bed. While I wouldn't recommend it to anyone, fight injuries are a fine way to expand your intellectual horizons. My list of books read has almost doubled. When my eyes get too tired to read, I watch a DVD. Robin actually moved the DVD player from her room into mine, and on occasion, we watch a movie together. Sometimes we both like the movie; sometimes not. We saw a DVD of this great Tim Burton movie called *Big Fish*; she hated the story about a son trying to understand his father's life, while I was bawling by the end.

When Kylee enters my room, a deep, gasping breath leaves my body. I wish the world would suddenly change to black-and-white, but Kylee remains a gray area, no matter what color her hair. She's at her most beautiful, like the first time I saw her over a year ago. The only difference is that her violet hair has been replaced by her natural chestnut color.

"Hello, Bret," she says, having the smarts to retire "cutie."

"K," I whisper, motioning for her to sit down, then I sip water so I can try to speak.

"How are you doing?" she says, gently stroking the side of my face, since there's no hair for her to put her fingers in, no ponytail to pull playfully.

"Ok," I say, my volume still low. The pain of Hitchings's punches was mild in comparison to the blows now hammering my heart and soul.

"Is it hard for you to talk?" she asks. "That's a first. I'll have my mom alert the media."

I laugh, which hurts but not as much as these visions of Kylee filling my eyes.

She sighs as she looks around my room. "Bret, when are you going to get a computer?"

I manage the patented Hendricks shrug.

"How will I keep in touch with you? How will you send me news of your plays and your band?" She scratches her head, and smirks. "Promise me you'll work on that, okay, kid?"

I smile as best as I can, but the thought of staying in Kylee's life overwhelms me because I never wanted to leave it. But I'm not sure if I'm ready to enter it again in a supporting role. Even with her sitting here now, I don't know where I stand with her and with my own heart.

"Early happy birthday!" she opens up a small bag, taking out a box of Godiva chocolates and a pack of clove cigarettes. She puts them next to the table, then turns away. Broken eardrum or not, I know that sound. It's Kylee crying, not for attention, but out of affection. "I remember when you got those for me on my birthday, and I didn't appreciate them," she says, not even trying to hold back tears now. "Just like I didn't appreciate you."

I hold her hand, so much smaller than mine, yet it still seems a perfect fit. "It's okay."

"Bret, I'm so sorry about Sean," she says softly, although I finally hear her clearly.

"It's okay, I forgive you," I whisper. Everyone is sorry. Sean couldn't help falling in love with her, any more than I could. Life isn't fair. Accept it. Move on. I still think about why, but I try to focus on what's next. Forgiving all three of us catapults me forward.

"Something else," she says, handing me the letter I wrote on her eighteenth birthday. "I want you to have this. I hope somebody else makes you this happy again. I'm sorry that I—"

I clutch her tiny hands, trying to return the letter, but she pulls away, reaching into her bag and pulling out her purple journal. "I want you to have this."

My eyes open wide, and my jaw would drop if it hadn't recently been wired shut. "Kylee, I . . ." I can't go on. The few words I've spoken to her have injured and exhausted me.

She gets up from her seat and walks away from me, then comes back with my metal trash can and empties its contents on the floor. "And I want you to have this."

She hands me her old Dr. Evil lighter, then she speaks through tears. "Burn it! Bret, burn it! I don't want either of us to remember me as being as evil as I was to you. I'm so sorry."

I take the journal, but I don't drop it into the trash can. Instead I open it to my morning of mourning. She's left the evidence there, and I wonder why. I take out the Polaroid documenting how I erased her name from the concrete and place it into her hands.

She kneels by the bed, then lowers herself slowly and gently onto my chest. It hurts, but I don't mind. After a long silence, she says, "Bret, I'm so sorry that I hurt you. I loved you, but it wasn't enough. I wanted to always have that feeling of *falling* in love, not just *being* in love. It's like when you're dancing, and the best part is waiting for the music to start, the anticipation before you go flying through the air. I guess I wanted love to be like that: just the fun part. I wish I could change how I behaved, but I can't. I just never want to be that way again."

"It's okay," I whisper, running my hands over her hair, and then handing her back her letter. "But keep this because—"

"It's the real thing." She slips easily back into finishing my sentences. She looks down at the letter, strokes the side of my face again, and then puts it into her small violet purse. Kylee's reckoning isn't about revenge, but learning never to forget, for all the right reasons.

I hug her, then drop the journal into the metal trash can she set by the side of the bed. Kylee holds the Polaroid in front of me and I know what I must do. I flick the Dr. Evil lighter, but it doesn't ignite the first time; it takes a couple tries to get it right. Finally, it connects, and the picture goes up in flames. My unkind deed becomes kindling as I drop it in the trash on top of the purple journal, which begins to turn into black-and-white ashes as we torch those memories good-bye. I take my water bottle from the table next to the bed and get ready to extinguish the flames.

Thirty-two

July 14, Before Senior Year

Where's Dad?"

It's the question I've been posing all weekend, but Mom refuses to give me a straight answer. She sent Robin over to Cameron's trailer, but from the tired look in her eyes, she hasn't sent herself to bed. Now it's late Monday afternoon, and he's nowhere to be seen.

"I don't know Bret, I don't know," she says, regaining her composure long enough to express her confusion. She keeps her hands in her pockets, trying to hide the nervous tremble.

"He's coming to this, right?" I ask as we sit outside of Morgan's office. Mr. Walker is inside already, conferring with Morgan. Bob Hitchings's father is late.

"Bret, I fear the worst," Mom says, unable to look at me. "It's been almost seventeen years since he's disappeared like this. It was the weekend before you were born."

I look up at my mom, wondering what she's trying to tell me.

"He went on a three-day drunk, showing up at the hospital barely able to stand. I told him that was it. He either quit drinking or he'd lose his family, including you, his newborn son. Your grandfather drove him home, and I don't know what he said, but your father never drank again after that. Your grandfather was a real hard man. A bastard, really, but you know, that weekend I'm glad he was. Sometimes you've got to be hard to make life easier for someone else."

Her words—"You've got to be hard to make life easier for someone else"—explode in my ears.

"I'm afraid that he's drinking again," she continues. "You don't know how stressful this has been for us. I know you've had a hard year, but you have no idea what we've gone through."

"I'm sorry," I say.

"I'm really scared." She looks at her watch. Both fathers are missing in action. Funny, how I've been missing my father for a long time, when he's been there in front of me all along.

"He'll be here," I say, trying now to be an empathy machine for her.

"We had a fight on Friday night," she says.

"I didn't hear—"

"It was in the garage. I told him things I should have told him long ago, about how he treats you, and the things you've been going through. He doesn't know about you, Bret, and it hurts him. He used to think that you hated him, just like he hated his dad."

"But—"

Mom interrupts me. "He didn't know how close you were to getting expelled from school. I finally told him. I couldn't protect him or you any longer. He didn't know how—"

"Hard it's been for me?" I butt in, recalling past years, not past months. "He made it harder."

"Should he have asked you? How? For so long, you didn't talk to him. Bret, he's so proud of you, and he's so ashamed of himself." She looks at her watch, as if she could will my father there.

All those years of holding back, no wonder he ran off into the night.

"Mrs. Hendricks, Bret, please come inside," Mr. Walker says, motioning us into the very conference room I'd once vowed never to enter again. We sit down, but I notice that Morgan is staying in his office, door closed. "Mr. Hitchings won't be joining us today."

"What?" Mom asks with mild surprise.

"It seems your husband and Mr. Hitchings agreed this morning to settle this matter between themselves," Walker says as I try to imagine Dad fighting Mr. Hitchings in a father's prom rematch.

"What do you mean?" my mom asks, equally confused.

"Your husband said he'd explain when he got here."

"And what about me?" I ask.

"Again, I'll let your father explain when he arrives."

My mom and Mr. Walker small talk for a while until Dad finally knocks on the door. He enters but it doesn't look like him—I've never seen him in a suit before—and he's not alone. Standing next to him is a man in an expensive charcoal gray suit. "Dad, what's going on?"

He ignores the question and asks impatiently, "Are we set here? What do we sign?"

Walker pushes some papers across the table but keeps a copy for himself. I look for the word *transfer,* but I can't see it. "Bret, you'll be going to school here next year," Walker says.

If I didn't have a broken mouth, I would scream for joy. Gray Suit Guy hands the papers to Dad. "I don't understand," Mom says, looking over at Dad.

"Explain it to them," Dad replies, sitting down next to me, while Walker reads aloud.

"The school district regrets the injuries that Bret Hendricks suffered while at an official school function, albeit one off-site." Walker starts talking in lawyerese, but this time I don't tune him out. "In addition, we have learned through students Alex Shelton, Will Kennedy, and Sean Dupont that Bret informed a teacher, a school counselor, and Principal Morgan that Bob Hitchings continually harassed both Bret and Alex, which led to the unfortunate incident at the prom, where Mr. Hitchings assaulted Mr. Hendricks."

I'm almost too stunned to speak. "What does—"

"Finish it," Dad says, cutting me off, while Gray Suit Guy stands behind him, unsmiling.

"Thus, Bret will not be expelled; in return, his family agree not to sue the district."

"Sue?" I mouth the words. Gray Suit Guy is a bloodsucker, and Morgan is his prey.

Walker isn't finished. "But since fighting at a school function is a serious and suspendable offense, Bret agrees to the following: first, that he will attend a weekly conference with Mrs. Pfeil."

I nod in agreement.

"Second, Mr. Douglas will act as Bret's official mentor."

"What does that mean?" I mumble.

"It's blackmail, but we'll take it," my father says, acknowledging Gray Suit Guy. "The deal is if you screw up one more time, then Mr. Douglas is going to take the hit. His fate is kind of in your hands. That's a lot of responsibility, but I figure you are up to it, right, Son?"

I again nod in agreement.

"Third, Bret will do fifty hours of community service at the North End Food Bank."

"Why . . . ?" I start.

"Just because you're not guilty doesn't mean you're not re-sponsible," Dad says.

"Finally, Bret, the school district takes no official position in the forthcoming litigation between your father and Mr. Barton Hitchings."

"What?" I ask my dad, but his eyes reveal nothing but stress and strain.

My father says nothing; he just nods at Gray Suit Guy. "We're done, right?"

"Right," Walker says, as my parents sign some papers. I walk out of the office, bewildered. Gray Suit Guy stays behind to chat with Walker, vampire to vampire.

"What was that about?" Mom asks as the three us finally walk toward the parking lot.

"At the hospital, Alex shared with me how Sean once told you the best way to get back at Hitchings was to let him beat you up and then sue him. I know that's not what you were thinking, but you take the hand you're dealt, right?" Dad says, opening the door.

"Riiiiiiiiiight." I throw in a little Dr. Evil to comment on Dad's good deed, but he doesn't smile. The somber look on his face is as dark as the ill-fitting suit he's wearing.

"Alex told me how you stood up for him, and how in your speech you stood up for what you believed in," Dad adds. "You got knocked down, but you got back up. Good job, Son."

"I just couldn't take it anymore," I say, looking only at the hard ground below.

"You should have come to me," Dad says, but we both know that used to be impossible. "I should have been there for you."

"You were there when I needed you," I manage to say, thinking back to the night in the garage after I lost Kylee, the day in his truck when he tried to warn me not to go back with her, and just now in the principal's office. "And you even used a lawyer to help. You hate lawyers."

"I do," Dad replies, pulling out his NASCAR key chain.

"I thought we didn't have any money to hire a lawyer," Mom says.

"Or to pay the hospital bills," Dad says, opening the Metro's passenger door for Mom.

"How can you sue Barton Hitchings without a lawyer?" Mom asks as her hands shake.

"Well, I hate lawyers, but everything has a place in this world," Dad admits.

My mother is concerned. "But how can we afford a lawyer and pay the hospital?"

"We should be able to pay some of the hospital bills and use this lawyer to sue that son of a bitch Bob Hitchings's father for the rest," Dad replies, his voice barely audible, like he's shrinking away. "We have enough money now."

"How?" I ask a split second before my mother.

Dad looks hard at the ground, then softly at me. "I sold the Camaro."

Thirty-three
July 25, Before Senior Year

Bret, hand me a nail."

"One second," I tell Mr. Douglas, wondering how he can hear me over the swirling sounds of my fellow thespians finishing the sets for the summer play. Will is out front as the lead, while I'm in back, giving me a whole new perspective. It'll be strange not to be the star of the show, but it feels good to be out of bed, back with friends, being part of something.

"Hey, stage manager, hurry up," Will says as he walks past. "I bet Becca's waiting for you!" I swallow another laugh thinking about taking over as stage manager after Kylee, and how my life's now about that very thing: taking over after Kylee.

"Okay, but I'll see you later," I tell Will, knowing I'll see him and Alex at band practice tonight. I shoot him a wave, then open up the bag of nails. I look through the nails to find one that's a little bent, a little different from the others. No doubt, it's been used before. I put it in my pocket as my last souvenir of Kylee.

"Here you go," I say, handing Mr. Douglas another nail, then helping him finish with the flat so I can exit the stage. I have to balance my time here with working my Chili's job, my hours at the Food Bank, recording the first Radio-Free Flint CD, and time with Becca.

"Thanks, Bret," Mr. Douglas says. We both seem to know that I'm almost Bret again.

"Ok, Mr. D.," I say with a smile, even if smiling still hurts sometimes. But I do it to remind myself that even months after Kylee betrayed me, I sometimes fear that I'll never laugh, love, or live again. Wrong. Wrong. Wrong. It's going to take a little bit of time and a whole lot of Becca's understanding. We're different on the outside, but deep down I think we believe in the same things. She knows who she is, while I'm still learning who I am and who I want to be.

"We're done!" Mr. Douglas says after a few more minutes of hard work, then lets out a satisfied sigh as he walks off the stage. As I connect the final pieces by hammering in the last nail, just a little off center, I think how life is better because we're connected to each other. I recall what Tom Joad said in *The Grapes of Wrath,* about how we're all part of something bigger. I think about how Mr. Douglas risked his job so I could finish out at Southwestern, but mostly I think about how Dad sold his precious Camaro to help me. Others have given to me, now I've got to find a way to give back.

"See you tomorrow, Mr. D.," I say as I give the nail a last gentle tap. My work is done here, at least for now. I'll drive myself home in Mom's Metro, its oil and my outlook freshly changed, stopping on the way to look at the words *Bret Lives* still staining Grand Trunk concrete. I'll sit there in my car, think about Becca, my senior year, Radio-Free Flint's new lineup, and my father, and I'll know those words are the fuel I'll use to make my own way on this human highway.